Charlotte

Charlotte

a Charlotte Smart Mystery

STAN CHARNOFSKY

HAWKSHAW PRESS, MILTON, DE

Charlotte: A Charlotte Smart Mystery is a work of fiction. All names, characters, places, and incidents are the products of the author's imagination, or are used fictitiously. Any resemblance to actual events, locales, businesses, or persons (living or dead) is entirely coincidental.

Hawkshaw Press
219 Milton Ellendale Highway
PO Box 491
Milton, DE 19968

Hawkshaw Press is an imprint of Devil's Party Press, LLC.
hawkshawpress.com

ISBN: 978-1-7340918-2-3

Library of Congress Control Number: 2021940381

Cover and book design by David Yurkovich.

Love forever to my real-life sister, Charlotte, who died two months before her 100th birthday.

SC

Old age hath yet its honor and its toil.

Alfred Lord Tennyson

Charlotte

1

HER FOREFINGER is thrust up into her left nostril. I watch with curious interest to see if she will do what little children do and lick the probing digit.

She is in her seventies, possibly eighty, white hair bristling and as unkempt as Edward Scissorhands.

An elevator is close quarters and she is not a child. For a moment she seems aware of possible eyes on her.

Surreptitiously, she moves the finger toward her mouth and the bare tip of her tongue slides through her lips and touches it.

Retreat; yet, in another few seconds, the tongue action is repeated.

I smile politely. Do we indeed return, as we reach the elder years, to our childhood urges? Well...of course, not all elderly folks do what she does. Charlotte wouldn't think of it.

Don't know the woman; will never see her again.

I am in New York, to catch a couple of shows before taking New Jersey Transit to Pennsylvania to visit my older sister who, I am certain, would be repulsed by my elevator companion's vulgar act.

I use the word *vulgar*, though aware that in some societies such behavior may not be considered repulsive at all. We are, admittedly, products of culture.

Charlotte is my sister, past sixty-five and growing. Well, of course one can grow at sixty-eight, or any age. Shaw was witty into his nineties; Churchill drank whiskey and smoked cigars into his; and then there was George Burns, who stayed with us for over one-hundred years, and who, when asked about his smoking, said that his doctors told him to quit, but he didn't listen to them, and now they're all dead.

My sister lives in a retirement village not far from the touristy town of New Hope, Pennsylvania, on the Delaware River. I believe she is the second-youngest person living there.

Our family spent several decades in that area, but, when I was a child, Mom and Dad hauled us all in their old, loaded-down, four-door Plymouth sedan–which I called the Green Beetle–to the golden and hopeful state of California. The first week in Los Angeles, alas, the Green Beetle was stolen and all its tires removed: hope not shattered, but shaken. After a few days, we got it back, and Dad admitted, red-faced, that he had gone into a factory and left the keys in the car. Who knew from car thieves?

My New York trip is exciting–for a few days. Then it feels frenetic. I'm a people watcher and the Big Apple is a bonanza of diverse, odd, eccentric, desperate, pitiful, interesting people.

But soon enough, I've had enough. My mind is elsewhere. After all, I am hopelessly in love and my chances of consummating my heart's desires are nil.

As I drive through Yardley Village on the Pennsylvania side of the Delaware, past the still-water Afton Pond where mallards and a couple of geese seem painted in the water and by the two-hundred-year-old, rectangular, redbrick library landmark, guarded near its entrance by two bronze sentinels that look like Benjamin Franklin–I am not alone.

It is a glorious feeling to be in among the maples and sycamores and oaks that turn the narrow country roads into shady and mysterious pathways. The Delaware flooded three years ago, rose over twenty feet, and inundated hundreds of riverside homes–which now have been rebuilt on raised platforms.

I say I am not alone, meaning I am with Meredith, a heavenly young woman who sees me as avuncular. I have designs on her–about as practical as having designs on Charlize Theron.

It was two years ago, during a previous Charlotte visit, when Meredith and I found each other. That is pretentious, I know, since she would likely deny having found me.

Meredith was thirty-one at the time, and I (Charlotte is seventeen years my senior) forty-nine–certainly a hefty spread between us, but not outlandish, not impossible to negotiate.

That time, I had rented a car, and drove through Yardley, past

Newtown and Langhorne, and on to Bigelow Village, where Char lives. The parking area near the entrance door to her complex was full but I spied an SUV pulling out and swerved my rented Toyota in at once. I heard violent honking and stepped out of my car to see a young woman leaning out her vehicle's window, screeching at me.

"What the hell! Didn't you see me waiting here? Just because she pulled out the other way doesn't give you priority!" Her left arm spun in frustrated circles.

"Oh," I said lamely. I liked her red-haired, green-eyed look, her high cheekbones, bare arms and thin fingers, and I also, of course, caught her fury. This was no retiring woman, giving in to a man's intrinsic rights; gender had nothing to do with it. The scold was on.

I am not a contentious person or, I believe, a chauvinist. As she berated me, I stepped away from my car, and, as I did, saw another auto, down the row, start to back out. My arm swung forward and I pointed with urgency (and relief): "Look! There's a place. Grab it quick!"

She did, and I waited, certain she would not be placated, expecting a verbal tirade as she came toward me, and the doorway.

Before she could say a word, I spread my hands out to the side and said, "I'm awfully sorry. Truly, I didn't see you. If there weren't another spot, I would have backed out and let you have mine."

"Fat chance," she said, with a nasty look.

It was early November, a brisk day but with azure skies, and the east coast autumn had already burned the deciduous tree-leaves to yellows, oranges and reds. A vagrant thought grabbed me that one ought not to be fuming on such an elegant day.

She strode past me and into the building—but not before my always beauty-seeking eyes checked out her trim figure and firm, muscular legs—a jogger, I decided.

At that time, two years ago, an irony occurred in that as Meredith was visiting her seventy-something-year-old grandmother, my visit to Charlotte was paired with a presentation she had asked me to make on "Growing Older, Or Older and Growing." Grandmother and Meredith were part of my audience of forty. That's what I do: I lecture and teach on a variety of family issues.

When my hour-long offering was over, several of the residents crowded around, two or three in wheelchairs, a couple more with walkers. Alongside was Meredith, guiding a wheelchair occupied by her grandmother, a substantial, white-haired woman with enormous blue eyes that stared straight ahead and tilted upwards. I could see that she was blind.

As the others peeled away, Meredith stepped up and said, in what I liked to think was a sheepish voice, "I enjoyed your lecture."

"Yes," her grandmother added. "Fine job, young man." She was wearing a knitted woolen sweater, cut wide to accommodate her ample body. It was open in front, and under it she wore a tie-dyed tee shirt, multi-colored and almost luminescent in its brightness.

Young man. When one is blind, certainly age has to be measured by energy, enthusiasm, and high spirit rather than looks. All at once, I felt wonderfully young.

"Thank you both," I said. "I'm flattered."

"Flattered is one thing," Grandmother said, "but I can tell you are an educated man, and I would guess you have presented in front of old fogies before."

I smiled. "I don't think of you as old fogies. I think of you as splendid survivors."

Meredith said softly, "I apologize for my harsh behavior in the parking lot."

I noticed that my sister Charlotte looked at us oddly.

"Oh no," I answered, "I did trespass. Your reaction was quite appropriate."

In that moment, we became friends, Grandmother Claire Hazelton, Meredith Hazelton, and I. Claire was an elderly person who, I was certain, would not, along with my sister, pick her nose and introduce the product into her parted lips. Something about her was magnetic, a genuineness, a munificent spirit that shown through those pale, unseeing eyes.

Charlotte told me later that the granddaughter was a frequent visitor, and that Claire was a sweet and sparkling woman who lost her eyesight some eight or ten years earlier as a result of macular degeneration, the more severe, wet kind, where blood collects behind the retina.

"I don't know Meredith," Charlotte told me, "but I do know that she is devoted to her grandmother. I consider Claire a lovely friend."

Before I returned home from that visit, Meredith and I exchanged emails and phone numbers. My foolish presumption was romantic in nature, while her purpose, I have since learned, was an interest in my work (I am a college teacher, specializing, as I said, in family relations), and a long-distance friendship that might enrich her.

Meredith was, and is, a licensed social worker, employed by Bucks County to work with indigent families, often with incidents of substance abuse. I know she is good at what she does, since her empathy is elegantly partnered with a keen intellect. I also know she can blow her top when crossed.

On this particular trip, she has picked me up at Hamilton Station in New Jersey, after my one-hour train ride from New York. This is not, however, a pleasant time.

Char had told me on the phone that Claire Hazelton had passed in the night, and now, a week later, I am arriving for my yearly visit. Meredith is clearly distraught, almost morose.

In the two years since Meredith and I became friends, I have learned that her father died when she was a child, and that her mother lived in Florida. Claire was her father's mother, and she and Meredith's mother did not get along. As I knew to expect, Meredith had to handle her grandmother's death all alone.

"It's a mess," she says, while motoring slowly along in the penumbra of arching maples and oaks. "Claire has been my rock, the only person I could feel totally safe with."

I wonder, in that tense moment, what Meredith has to feel unsafe about, but remain silent.

"All the stories about my different sucky relationships that I'd bombard her with were always received with patience and wisdom."

At that, I realize I am insanely jealous. I don't see her for months at a time, after all, and this is the first moment I realize that for all I know she may have a boyfriend, may be sleeping with someone, may be in love.

Since we met, she has come to California twice, once for a conference and the other time to visit an old high school friend who moved to LA ten years earlier and lives in Marina del Rey. Each time I invited her to stay in my townhouse, assuring her that I have a separate suite upstairs with private bath—and each time she gracefully declined and stayed with her friend instead.

After a quiet few moments, in which I take in the embracing ambience of Pennsylvania's autumn riches, she says, "You know, Greg, it's not that Grandmother didn't have issues of her own. I mean, she needed me as well, would tell me secrets that no one in the world could even imagine. We trusted each other."

Finally, I say, "You had a sweet connection. That's what makes it so painful."

"It's hard to explain, but she was my grandma *and* my sister, my true confidante. Crazy to put it this way, but she really understood me, was almost like a therapist to me. She had amazing listening skills."

I want to bellow to the trees: "I have those skills! Use me! With your grandmother gone, let me be your confidential ear!"

What I say is, "It's rare to find a person with that talent. And even more, the wisdom to know how to use it with her granddaughter."

We are nearing Bigelow Village (but not for me to lecture this trip—only my regular visit with Charlotte), driving past an enormous open field with a rain-caused lake, where hundreds of wild geese collect. In the pause of conversation I say to Meredith, "Char told me the geese used to fly far to the south in the fall, but now tend to stay local the year around." I find my mind occupied thinking about the birds, Meredith, other things I could say, and what I remember is my sister telling me:

"Those birds are dirty creatures, and in the spring, we have to be cautious because they cross the highway with their little trailing broods." But it seems an unkind piece of information to one who has just lost her grandmother, and so I stay in Meredith's silence.

The car rolls on, and after a few more quiet moments, Meredith says softly, almost inaudibly, over the hum of her car's motor, to herself as much as to me, "Claire was a murderer."

2

MEREDITH'S last-minute disclosure, while startling to me, was left hanging, as at that moment we drove into the Village parking area, and she dropped me off, turning toward me and saying, "I'll see you later. Hope your visit with your sister is lovely."

Meredith is correct. It is lovely to see Charlotte again. As usual, we pick right off where we left off the last time, and it's not too long before our talk turns to Meredith and the death of her aunt Claire.

"I don't understand it," Charlotte says, "I had a long talk with her a couple of days before, and she told me, though tired, she was feeling spirited. Limited, of course, in where she could go, but enjoying her friends and her meals, and listening to old ballads and classical music—Claire loved Sinatra and was a Beethoven devotee. I tell you, Greg, I was stunned when the word got around that she had passed."

My mind-set is to keep Meredith's revelation, if that is the proper word for it, to myself until she and I can discuss it. Alarming sort of information—and it was clear that when she uttered the words, she was struggling. But I can poke around about myself, and so I ask Char, "What does the doctor say? I mean, for the cause?"

"So far, all we know is that she died of natural causes. Since there is no hint of any kind of foul play, no autopsy has been called for. Claire had her idiosyncrasies, but most everyone here—those who knew her, maybe a hundred folks—seemed to appreciate her."

"Must be depressing with all the elderly folks here, to see them go. I mean, it's obvious that before long, many are going to die."

"That's the negative about living in a retirement community. I do enjoy the camaraderie, the food is okay, and the ambience is pleasant. But I miss the vigor of younger people. And I miss children."

Makes sense to me. Charlotte is elderly by societal standards, but her body is spry and spirited, and she is a lot like a child in her wonder, the way she scrutinizes a new concept or idea, not satisfied until she gets it. She even dresses colorfully, playfully, though in keeping with good taste. Her hair is grey and neat, and her eyes—those penetrating eyes—see a lot more than mine, even if mine are much younger.

"You and I seem to have eschewed having kids. Well, I haven't given up completely. Depends on whether I can find a young enough woman who is willing and still fecund."

Char makes a face at me. "Hmm. Upper-crust word, *fecund*. Not going to catch many of the young ones talking like that, not that I've noticed you looking too hard in any case."

I debate whether to tell her about my fixation on Meredith, and decide not to. Instead, I say, "Like sports stars, I'm holding out for a bigger bonus."

"Good luck. It's not about money; it's about an elusive thing called love."

Charlotte nails me all the time. Over my fifty or so years, I have been in love a couple of times, and I admit to being a bit stung when things haven't worked out, but then I seem to be able to get on with my life, alone. It makes her doubt my sincerity on the matter of wife and family.

Char and I are having lunch in the large eating hall in Bigelow Village, a room with a towering ceiling, bolstered with what I call flying buttresses, though I'm not sure what an architect would call them. There are windows on two sides, the kitchen area on the third, and the entrance from the hall on the fourth. Some forty tables are set around the spacious room, though on this day only perhaps twenty or so folks are having lunch. The food, Charlotte has told me, is acceptable but not gourmet. The menu has its standard daily fare, with specials on given days. The waiters are college students, and so one might expect the service to be spotty. It begs the question, then, of why Charlotte lives here.

"I don't eat fish," Charlotte says, "but I hear good things about the tilapia. I think I might order a melted cheese sandwich, maybe with some of their cold strawberry soup first. It's good, the strawberry soup."

A woman who is perhaps in her seventies approaches our table and sits at the third of four chairs. I see Char sort of frown slightly, then say, "This is Freda Graham. Freda, I'm not sure if you know my brother, Greg."

"Saw him last year and the year before," Freda says, in a high, whiny voice, but with a contrasting sparkle in her dark eyes. "Presented on growing older, and then on understanding our grandchildren. Thought it was odd since he–I mean *you*–didn't have any of your own."

"Well," I said, feeling defensive, "as a teacher, I don't always have to experience something to know about it."

"That is probably true, because I enjoyed both of your workshops."

"He's not presenting this time," Charlotte says. "Here just for the pleasure of our company."

"*Your* company," Freda says. "I can't imagine he–*you*–would relish the company of most of us old battleaxes."

I smile at her self-deprecation, and say, "Hard on yourself, aren't you?" aware that Claire, too, had once spoken negatively about the residents of Bigelow Village.

"Not at all. I'm blunt but truthful."

"Yes," Charlotte says, "Freda is our ultimate 'tell-it-like-it-is' resident. Got to pay attention to our veracity when she's listening."

"The only way to live," Freda says. "Now, poor Claire, she was an honest one, but you see it got her in trouble."

"Oh?" I ask, galvanized by the reference to Meredith's grandmother. "How did it get her in trouble?"

Charlotte smiles. I can see she knows, but waits for Freda's answer.

"Claire was proud of her atheism. Blind as a bat, she was, but her vision about a deity–or the lack of one–was clear as a bell. Made no bones about the fact that religion has been the cause of most wars."

Now I smile. My sister is so different from both Freda and the way she is characterizing Claire. Charlotte, I am sure, is a nonbeliever as well, but has not the remotest interest in evangelism. I would doubt that anyone in the entire village even knows her position on spiritual issues, though she is outspoken when it comes to politics and social inequality.

"So, you're saying that folks here resented her for...well, I guess you could say, her radical stance on religion?"

"You got it, Charlotte's brother. A lot of resentment. This is not a place where people want to be told they've thought the wrong thing their whole lives."

"But no one ever threatened her...?"

"I'm not so sure," Charlotte says. "She once told me of a nasty note she got, that her granddaughter read to her. It was camouflaged as to subject matter, but read something like, 'Disrespect for eternal matters is ignorance.' She said she tossed it."

A man, using a walker, slides toward our table, a wrinkled grin spreading. Before he arrives, Char says softly, "Elmore. His wife is here too."

"You must be the kid," Elmore says to me. "I have three kids and four grandchildren."

Freda scowls at the intrusion, but Char says, "And you also have a great-grandson."

"I do?"

"Yes," Freda says with annoyance, "and you always forget about him."

"Oh." He smiles vaguely and slides his walker away and toward the entrance, where his wife is summoning him with a waving arm.

"The wife there is a first-class religious freak," Freda says as she stands, "and he's just out of it; wouldn't know religion from pizza. Well, good to see you, teacher. Sorry you won't be holding forth this year. When you come again, I have a good topic for you: How to be happy despite living with decrepit old farts."

As she stomps away, Char says, "You can see she's an iconoclast. Elmore has Alzheimer's, and Freda can't stand him."

"She has strong opinions for certain, and you do have your characters here. Makes me realize, even more, how different we all are."

Charlotte is quiet for an instant, then says, almost to herself. "Yes, that's right. Claire was a target for people insulted by her beliefs." She hesitates, and says to me, "She was buried a few days ago, but I wonder if it would be possible to exhume the body and do an autopsy?"

"What? Are you saying you believe there was foul play of some sort? Here?"

"You know Greg, we're none of us dead yet, and we still have our passions."

"I'm sorry, Char. I know you do."

"Well, if she was 'done away' with, she has the right to justice, no matter how old she was. But no one is ever going to suggest they check. I wonder, Greg, do you think I can get the police to listen to me?"

"I think you're one of the most astute people I know, Char. So I say, 'Hey, Ms. Marple, go for it!'"

—

Charlotte is roundly appreciated at Bigelow Village for her helpful attitude with and toward other residents. Since she is younger than most and still filled with energy, she reads to those in the more intensive care units—articles from the *New York Times* or short fictional stories—at least a couple of times a week. She also gets paid ten dollars for accompanying an elderly person to a doctor's appointment, pushing the wheelchair, helping them in and out, providing moral support.

The fact that she now suspects some sort of foul play with Claire's death gets me to wondering about her own safety.

We are in her unit, a one-room apartment with an open kitchen and small bathroom; it is light and airy, and the large bay window looks out on fall colors and a gently rolling expanse of still dark, green grass. As I gaze out, I can almost smell the wonderful fragrance of the recently mowed lawns.

"So, Char, if you believe Claire's death was not natural, aren't you concerned that there is a dangerous person living here? I mean, you'd think that people in their seventies and eighties would have settled into a sort of harmony, and made peace with the ironies of life."

"There are loonies at every age and in every corner. But yes, it would be a good idea to find out if we're dealing with one here."

"Claire was pretty well liked, and you are too. So, what does that say about who could be targeted next?"

"Not exactly what I meant to suggest by 'looney,'" she says, while turning off the gas under the whistling kettle, "this could be a one-time vendetta, the cause of which is still obscure. But, in my view, anyone who kills another is not normal."

She bustles about in the kitchen area and says, "You like green tea, do you not? High in antioxidants. And I have a nice coffeecake for dessert." She laughs, her cute little laugh which I have learned to appreciate, and adds, "It comes from one of my favorite mixes."

All this conjecture about foul play and vendettas stirs me to want to get back to Meredith and her awful pronouncement in the car.

What could she have meant about her grandmother being a murderer? Did she mean it literally? And if so, well yes, a vendetta could certainly be the cause for Claire's unexpected exit.

Charlotte, more perceptive than I ever considered, says suddenly, "Greg, I don't expect you to have dinner with me tonight. The granddaughter, Meredith, is, I know, high on your agenda. So, go enjoy yourself—but nosey as I am, I will want a full report when I see you next."

I hug her. I don't see her as nosey. In my eyes she is always my caring, insightful, vigorous, intrepid, probing, and big sister.

Plan settled, after the tea and coffeecake, I call Meredith to pick me up—which she has offered to do—and take me to my nearby motel, called the Blue Dolphin, only a couple of miles from Bigelow Village.

Over the phone I say, "I have some curious news for you—and I really am eager to understand more about what you told me about Claire." I wait for an instant, and, when she says nothing, I tack on, "Are you willing to tell me? I mean, is that okay with you?"

"Not only okay," she replies. "I *must* tell you, but not on the phone."

I wait out the ten minutes until Meredith gets to me with my sister, both of us quietly thinking our own thoughts on the matter of Claire, though neither saying so out loud.

3

SINCE WE know each other well, Meredith coming into my motel room is not suggestive, nor does she see it as a ploy on my part to seduce her–though I'd be willing to shout to the Canadian geese out by the rain-made lake that I'd *love* to seduce her, that is, if she were willing. Which she is not.

The room is small but pleasant. A sign outside tells potential inhabitants that this is The Blue Dolphin–A Pleasant Place to Lose Your Blues. We sit on the edge of the bed, she at the foot, I at one side, and she begins.

"As a young woman, Grandma Claire had been, of all things, a police officer. No, I'm serious. When a person is in her seventies, you can't always tell the circuitous routes she took to get there. She was respected as a ballsy babe who passed near the top of every milestone on the training list at the police academy. But she had one thing that was an albatross around her neck."

She stops and I see that she is laboring internally with some dark secrets. I wonder why she said that she 'must' tell me all this.

"Your sister knew this about Grandmother, but as Claire told me, and this is a true compliment, 'Charlotte Smart is the most respected person in the complex, and abhors gossip.'"

"One thing," I repeat, "that was a burden for Claire...?"

"Yes. And that is that she was a lesbian. Oh, she was once married, and did have a couple of children. But all of it went against what she called her true nature. Well, you can imagine how being a lesbian would go over for a policewoman. Every cop in the precinct thought she was attractive and wanted to get into her pants. And when she would turn them down, they would broadcast that Hazelton was a queer."

"She had children, but realized she was gay and then…what, got divorced?"

"That's right, and I never knew my grandfather, not even sure he's alive. Claire turned seventy-four last summer; not too old, but since she's been blind for several years, decided she'd be better off in a residential facility. You know, she was a policewoman till her early forties, already single, a caring parent to her kids, and a damned target of every horny cop in Simi, California. She finally sued for harassment, and actually won a settlement. But, because of the hostility, decided she had better resign. A small pension came in monthly."

"How did she get here, in Pennsylvania?"

"My mother and I lived here, and, after Dad died, we hung around for a few years—I was in my teens—and Mom decided to move to Florida. I didn't want to leave my high school pals, had a boyfriend I thought I was in love with, so stayed with some friends till I graduated, then moved out on my own. When Claire left the police force, she lived with her partner, who was also an ex-cop, in California for nearly twenty years. They broke up when her eyesight began to go bad. She was past sixty, and she wrote to me asking if there was a good care facility near where I lived."

"All this is background. You have a sordid part still to tell."

"Yes. This part I didn't even know till about a year ago, and I decided it wasn't to anyone's benefit to make it public. One of those homophobic cops, while out on patrol with Claire, tried to rape her. As it happened, they had been sitting on a possible hold-up call for several minutes, and just as the partner attacked her, the perp ran from this liquor store. Claire fought her partner off, but during their struggle, he hit her on the head with his pistol, not enough to knock her out, but enough to stun her. He then leaped from the black and white and ordered the perp to freeze. The guy was almost on top of him and managed to bowl the cop over, and the two of them were rolling on the pavement when Claire exited the car, picked up the suspect's gun, and demanded he stop. The other cop then stood and without a word, shot the perp in the chest. The way Claire described it, she was so pissed at the cop, she fired the perp's gun at him. So, it was a murder for a murder. The fingerprints were not the issue, because it was the perp's gun that killed the cop, and vice-versa."

"Holy shit!" I say. "That's a movie of the week."

"Claire told me all this with great regret, as if she had gotten away with something and deserved punishment. Maybe she did, but, as you can imagine, I wasn't about to turn her in."

"Okay, so—even though I'm honored—why do you think I 'must' know all this?"

"Because I think my grandmother was killed. And I think your sister, Charlotte, is the one person here who can figure out how and why."

—

We do go to dinner, a Chinese restaurant Meredith knows with fierce, painted dragons on the wall and a large shield just inside the entryway. A fish tank is set near the reception counter, with bubbling water and at least ten exotic small fish, two bright blue with yellow tails, one a brilliant red. The host ambles up and says without us asking, "A Filipino man designed the tank with all the unusual flora. He is brilliant but unreliable. If something goes wrong, he is never available. Those two dappled fish, that hover in the tentacles of that odd-looking plant almost never leave there, because the other fish chase them. The plant has sharp thistles that bother the others, but not those two. There is also a baby eel, but it hides under the coral."

The food is okay—I like the crispy noodles and dip—but in all truth, the conversation is better. It is like a bonus to sit across from Meredith and, careful not to stare, look into that Technicolor countenance, with the dancing green eyes and rose-colored cheeks, and, of course, the striking, reddish hair.

"But, I still don't understand how in this faraway locale—at least far away from Simi Valley, California—anyone from the past would catch up to Claire. And if not from the past, then who would be so pushed out by her beliefs that he or she would want to kill her?"

"That's the mystery. Your sister is tuned into just about everyone here, and I'll bet she can identify who might be so offended. Besides that, she knew Grandmother quite well, and I am almost sure was in on much of her history."

"My little-big sister, Charlotte, on the inside of a full-blown whodunit! Wow! I always knew she was crafty, but a sleuth, a wannabe private eye? No way."

"That's what you have to do, now, Greg. Find out from your sister who she might suspect." She stops, and adds, in a most appealing way, "For me. Aside from her blindness, Claire was a sturdy woman. I need to know the truth about her death."

I want desperately to say, "Anything for you, Meredith!" but instead and as usual, I reply, "Of course. I'll see Charlotte tomorrow morning. It's Saturday, and you can come with me. We can...cross-examine her together."

"She doesn't know me very well. Might be she'd speak more freely to you alone."

I hesitate, aware that my request is for me, my need to be in Meredith's company, and say, "I don't think so. And anyway, I'd like for you to know her better."

She smiles—I think she wants to be there but doesn't want to seem as if she's pushing—and places her hand on my forearm. Grand moment! With a demure shyness Meredith says, "Okay, if you insist."

A one-way fixation is the most frustrating experience. As a sometimes counselor, I know we cannot live our lives on "if only." But, damn it, if only Meredith could *see me*.

4

I TELL CHAR that Meredith and I would like to take her out for breakfast. Her reply is instantaneous: "I usually have a bagel and coffee, so that would be a treat. Pick me up at nine o'clock."

We do, and as we are getting into Meredith's car, Char says to her, "Don't know why you and I never spent some time together. I really loved your grandmother. She and I had a special connection."

"I know that. She spoke of you often." Meredith pauses and adds, "She felt that you really understood her."

"In some ways, a complicated person," Char answers. "Her life was a challenge, but she handled it with grace. And by the way, she spoke of you often, too."

As we are about to close the last door, a woman taps one of the windows with her cane, making a rather solid clanking sound.

"Whoa," Meredith says.

"Where you going?" the woman asks.

Charlotte rolls down her window. "Trudy, this is my brother and that is Claire's granddaughter. They're taking me out to breakfast."

"It's too early," Trudy replies.

"Well, it's after nine. Some people get up early, you know."

"I don't eat breakfast. It sits on my stomach. I take my vitamins with prune juice, that's all."

"That's nice, Trudy. See you later."

"Claire died, you know."

"Yes," Charlotte says. "Bye now."

Meredith drives away and Charlotte says, "Believe it or not, Trudy is ninety. Her memory isn't so good anymore, but she is a determined woman with very strict rules."

"I could see that," I say.

"Hope she didn't crack my window."

"No," Charlotte says. "It was a wooden cane. She is a butt-in person. I mean she doesn't respect private conversations."

"Where shall we go for breakfast? What's a good place around here?" I ask.

"Tell you what," Char says with a whimsical look, "how about if we drive about fifteen minutes into New Hope. It's early enough so not too many tourists are there. A favorite spot of mine is Wally's—and I'll tell you another reason for going there. It was Claire's favorite too."

"She never told me," Meredith says, a wound in her voice.

"It was sort of her secret. Since she always needed transportation, she would whisper to me when no one was near, 'How about Wally's tomorrow morning?' And I would nod and go pick her up and off we'd drive."

"Must have been a chore for you," Meredith says.

"Oh, I'm used to pushing wheelchairs—and of course hers folded and I could put it into my car. She was a closeted French Roast coffee connoisseur, your grandma."

"What is so special about Wally's?" I ask.

"Aside from excellent coffee and a variety of omelets—and a great list of wines if you dine later in the day—Wally himself is special. I want you both to meet him. He was very nice to Claire."

"Wally's it is," Meredith says toward the windshield.

Meredith is vulnerable and adaptable. She gets insulted, yet seems to recover quickly. The loss of her grandmother is a heavy burden, and her eyes, still amazingly green and deep, seem to have lost a bit of their luster.

Her route takes us past Peddler's Village, an upscale shopping area a couple of miles from New Hope, located along gently rolling hills, it boasts three or four good restaurants and two yummy, quick-serve spots: a coffee store with pastries and gourmet brews, and a parlor serving the richest and creamiest of ice creams. Char and I had landed in Peddler's Village a couple of times in past years to partake of the goodies—and also to buy a certain kind of yarn and patterns she needed for her needlepoint. On this morning, we can already see a crowd gathering for what is clearly a classic car exhibit, something that does not attract me, so I am happy we are only passing through.

In New Hope we luck out and Meredith finds a parking spot on the main street only a hundred yards from a funky sign hanging on heavy ropes that reads, Wally's: The Brew for You, with an accompanying slogan below proclaiming, Nutrition for The Heart-y.

We enter an unpretentious vestibule area—on the West Coast we rarely have them since the weather never gets too cold—through one door and then a second, which on this day is open. The interior is gaily colored, with whimsical paintings on the walls ceiling, each looks as if rendered by children. I note this, to which Charlotte replies, "They were painted by Wally's kids. They're grown now, but they helped decorate the place when they were younger. Neat, isn't it?"

Soon Wally, himself, approaches us, menus in hand. "Well, Charlotte, I am delighted to see you—though it saddens me that you are without your sweetheart of a companion." He catches his words, and quickly adds, "Not that your present friends aren't welcome."

"Wally, this is Claire's granddaughter, Meredith, and this is my little brother, Greg Smart."

"Ah, all part of the family. Come in, come in. I have a lovely table for you that looks out on the fall colors and the Delaware Canal."

His almost gushy manner is a bit too much, but I trust Charlotte's judgment that he is truly caring.

Following coffee, Charlotte places both hands on the table and says, "I need to tell you something. I went to the hospital unit last evening, and tracked down the doctor who was called when Claire passed. His name is, of all things, Doolittle, Dr. Frederick Doolittle. He was most accommodating, and I came away with some useful information."

"Information that we didn't know before?" Meredith asks, her voice high and troubled.

"Well, yes, because I don't think the right questions were asked."

"Such as?" I ask.

"Such as...where was Claire when she was...uh, discovered? We knew she died in the night, but there were no specifics about her body's location. I presume everyone obviously expected that she died in bed, but Doolittle said no. She died in the bathroom. When her caretaker came to get her in the morning, she was curled up on the bathroom floor. The doctor told me that his first reaction was to search for a wound, in case she might fallen and hit her head. But there was none. Doesn't mean she couldn't have simply passed out on the toilet and collapsed from a heart attack or maybe even a cerebral hemorrhage."

"Wait a minute, Charlotte. Are you saying my grandmother fell on the bathroom floor and…and maybe was alive for a time?"

"The doctor didn't know that. She did, however, expire there and not in her bed."

"And since the apartment was locked and all that," I say, "there was no reason to think of any foul play. It was simply, as they say, her time?"

"Yes and no. No one did anything to her in that immediate span of time, but Dr. Doolittle, when I pushed a bit, admitted that a build-up of toxins in her body could have been introduced over time, and by another person. He, the doctor, of course, had no reason to believe anybody wanted to hurt Claire, so his examination was rather routine, and he reported that she died of natural causes. Unfortunately, that is the procedure too often with the elderly: an attitude of 'Oh well, she was old and ready to go.'"

"'Rage, rage against the dying of the light,'" I say, quoting Dylan Thomas.

"But, what can be done now to see if that theory about toxins is true?" Meredith asks.

"I asked the doctor about exhuming the body for an autopsy; while he was skeptical, he did not dismiss it. Instead, he said that if a family member requests it, and there is even a remote possibility of treachery, it could be done. It would take a court order."

Our food is delivered by a smiling young woman who is thorough, prompt, and absolutely accurate in every detail. Char grins at what I am sure is the contrast from the kids who serve her daily at Bigelow.

Wally checks on us, and we nod in appreciation of the tasty food. I admit sneaking intermittent glances at Meredith; assertive and outspoken as she is, her eating habits are delicate, almost dainty, and I wonder at her parental influence in that. One of my strong aversions is to people who eat ugly, especially with their mouths open. I see ballplayers on TV chewing with open mouths all the time, and I sometimes yell at the screen, "Your momma didn't teach you right!" My private obsession.

"I think we should raise the coffin," Meredith says. "Grandmother's death needs to be explained."

Charlotte's head bobs up and down. "I agree. Knowing Claire as I did, the unusual nature of her death makes little sense."

It is time to pay our check, and I am reminded of some reading I did a few weeks earlier. In the seventeenth century–the time of Descartes–in Sweden, during the reign of King Gustav Adolph, a monetary unit, a coin, was typically the size of a dinner plate, unwieldy and made of copper. The culture used mainly a barter system, taxes paid to the King in the form of cattle, oats, and hides.

We've come a long way, yet our typical barter unit today is an intrinsically nonvaluable piece of plastic–though to be sure, eventually we must cough up the green stuff, also only symbolically valuable.

On this day, in New Hope, Pennsylvania, Wally Burt does not let us pay a penny for our meal.

"A tribute to Claire," he says. "You know this, Charlotte; she was my favorite. Blind and all, she saw more than most people with twenty-twenty."

I realize, in this moment, that Wally is a man with uncommon nostalgia, or at least a soft spot for those with disabilities. I hadn't noticed, but now do, that he has one blue eye and one a pale, faded gray–that Wally has vision in only one eye.

He motions our server over and says, "Don't know if you ever met my eldest. This is Jessica, my daughter." Jessica turns shy, and says softly, "It was a pleasure serving you."

Wally hugs each of us when we leave–even me, which is okay, since in my line of work we do it often.

I leave a ten-dollar bill for Jessica, and as we walk in the cool mid-day air of this charming little hamlet, Meredith says, "Hard for me to absorb that grandmother never clued me in about this place, about Wally."

Charlotte says, as she waves to a gentleman across the street, "Claire was a most private person in many ways, and had the capacity to compartmentalize her life. That is why, I am certain, I knew so little about you. She was discrete and completely confidential." She stops, then calls out, "Hello there, Delbert!"

The man is close to elderly, perhaps a bit younger than Charlotte, and is sitting at the entrance to a women's clothing shop, smoking a pipe and reading a newspaper. He waves back and hollers loudly, "Hey there, honey, got your whole entourage with you today! Except for Claire. Awful about her going out like that."

"You know a lot of people, Sis," I say.

"Delbert Kraus owns Go Fur It!, which is a misnomer, because he won't sell animal fur. All his clothing is woven wool or cotton, with some faux fur trims. The store's name is a come-on. I've met his wife, too, Evangeline, an introverted and sad person. Delbert and Wally are like neighborly business colleagues."

"Seemed to know Claire," Meredith says.

"Uh…yes," Charlotte says absently, her mind elsewhere. Periodically, Charlotte will seem to turn inward as if pondering some elemental issue, as if working to figure out some distant conundrum. I'm sure it's what makes her such a keen problem solver.

We spend a moment taking in the art treasures of this charming resort town on the Delaware River, and at our return to our car I say, "What bewilders me is who in hell would want to harm Claire."

My wise sister replies, "Clandestine acts are often the products of warped minds. It does little good to apply logic to dementia."

When she says dementia, my thoughts immediately go to a good percentage of the population of Bigelow Village. Certainly not all, but some, of the elderly living there suffer some form of dementia. That notion puts a whole new twist on the mystery.

We motor slowly through the main street, now filling with tourists, and as we drive out of town, Charlotte says as if to herself, "…saw more than most people with twenty-twenty."

5

IN THE AFTERNOON, I decide to take a nap and Charlotte invites me to do it in her small apartment. Lying there, my mind churns and I pick up that in her last, almost laconic statement, was an implication that Claire may have seen–in a figurative rather than ocular sense–something that threatened someone.

When Meredith dropped us off, she agreed to come by in the morning so that she and Charlotte could address this Dr. Doolittle about an autopsy. Char still owns a Honda Civic and drives in the local area, to the market or sometimes chauffeuring a friend or two to a movie, or, as with Claire, to their cherished breakfasts at Wally's in New Hope. She drives me back to the Blue Dolphin Motel at 10:00 PM. I watch an old Hitchcock thriller on TV, which, not surprisingly, stirs my thoughts even more about Claire.

Later, I notice that my room phone is blinking red. I retrieve a message: "Greg, I don't believe I have appropriately thanked you for all you–and Charlotte too–are doing for me. I do enjoy you so much. You are a rich part of my life. See you in the morning."

Well, that sort of message is damned frustrating! Yes, Meredith enjoys me, and I know exactly how much and in what way. It's all so monitored, so regulated.

As I prepare for sleep, a nagging idea creeps in and hovers about me. The tale Meredith told about Claire's early career as a police-

woman, her lesbianism, the shooting, her partner, and then the disso-
lution when her eyesight failed—all that seems incomplete. Who was,
or is, that partner, and, when it ended, where did she go? Could someone from California have followed Claire here, and, if so, was she
aware? A long and intimate relationship is not likely to be completely
corrupted if there is love and affection. I know a lot of gay couples in
California, and their love is powerful cement, even when illness occurs. I make a mental note to query Meredith about this—though I
doubt she has the answers. My final thought before dozing off is that
if Meredith doesn't know, I'll bet Charlotte does.

—

Dr. Frederick Doolittle is a rotund fellow, pleasant, a fixed smile
on his cherry-tinted face, the farthest thing from Rex Harrison, who
played the good doctor in the first Dr. Doolittle movie, or Eddie Mur-
phy, who played him in the remake. His amiability is immediately apparent, as Charlotte introduces him to Meredith and me.

"As I understand it, you believe the woman who died last week
might have been the object of some dastardly intentions. Let's see
now, the name was...we've had two deaths in the past week...uh,
Claire Hazelton. Ah yes, the bathroom. Seemed peaceful enough...no
marks, no struggles, hardly seemed like foul play."

"She was perfectly healthy, Doctor, and, in fact—aside from her
blindness—enviously vigorous. She could get weary, but seemed always to push through with energy," Charlotte says, herself completely
amiable. I can see she is currying the good doctor, carefully avoiding
any criticism.

"Yes, yes, well that's the thing with geriatric populations. Genetic
predisposition steps in at any time, and nobody knows when or how.
I don't hold to destiny, but sometimes even I have to allow that a
person's time has come."

"Ms. Hazelton's niece, here, has reason to believe—since she has
inside information on history and relationships, and possible insults
one way or the other—that it may not have been a natural death. So,
the family is officially requesting an autopsy."

"I see. Yes, well, that certainly is possible. Let me set the wheels
in motion. I'll need you to fill out some forms, and write down what
has led you to desire such a radical request."

Meredith does what Doolittle asks, as Charlotte and I wander about the examination room, a room Charlotte knows, as the residents are seen here whenever an illness of any kind arises. She pauses at a cabinet with a glass-paneled door as if reading the labels of the many medicines within. I notice there is a keyhole in the cabinet that, I am certain, only the doctors may access.

"How many doctors work at Bigelow?" I whisper.

"I believe there are three or four. They rotate times and days, and no one is here more than five or six hours in a row, since they all have private practices."

"Any specialists? I mean like urologists or proctologists? Or maybe even internists?"

"I don't know their specialties. I'm sure each has one. Dr. Doolittle likes to broadcast that he is a general practitioner."

Meredith finishes with the forms and we thank the doctor. As we are about to exit the clinic, Charlotte says, "Doctor, would you have a record of the medications or supplements Ms. Hazelton was taking?"

Amazing! My sister seems to know exactly the critical things to ask.

"Oh," Doolittle mumbles. "Well, Overstreet was her regular doctor, but, of course, all the files are here. As next of kin, young Ms. Hazelton, here, certainly can peruse them."

"How about if we get you a photocopy of her medications and treatment over the past six months or so," Charlotte persists.

"Give me a moment, and I'll get the nurse to copy what you want."

After another ten minutes, we are walking toward Charlotte's apartment and Meredith says, "He's a nice fellow, a bit preoccupied, or maybe diffident."

"Just his style," Charlotte replies. "I've actually seen him irritated, primarily when he feels disrespected. I show him a lot of respect."

The hallway from the medical area of Bigelow to where Charlotte's apartment is located is as long as a city block. One may stand at the beginning and peer down an extended tunnel that seems to go on forever. We turn off, however, after only fifty feet, to the right, then through an automatic door that requires a tap on a silver wall cylinder to be activated. We pass through a lounge area with an outside door that leads to the parking lot, then up a small elevator to the second floor. Charlotte's rooms are only ten steps from the elevator.

In her apartment, our hands around mugs of steaming green jasmine tea, Charlotte says, "Overstreet is a different kind of cat. Doolittle can be soft and accommodating, but Overstreet tends to resent anyone questioning his approach or his diagnoses. The few times I've seen him for an ailment, I came away with a sense of his resentment of elderly people."

"He must be pretty young himself," I say. "If he were up in years, he would certainly not have an age bias."

"Right on, brother. Lyle Overstreet is barely forty. I think he is frustrated in his private work, and reluctantly sees patients here because he needs the extra income."

"But, since he was grandmother's primary caregiver, the question is, was he a good doctor and, if so, did he miss something? And if he did, why?"

"Unanswerable at this time, but maybe not forever," Charlotte says, a peculiar little gleam in her eye.

"What are you going to do with Claire's medical records?" I ask.

"I have a friend," she says, and I almost expect her to add, "the better to eat you with, my dear," or something else inscrutable.

"Yes…" I interject, drawing the word out.

"…whom I trust implicitly. He is my pharmacist, Oscar Ott. Some folks here call him Double O. I get all my prescriptions through him, and I'm certain that Claire did too—except, of course, if the doctor had samples to pass out."

"Samples?" Meredith asks.

"All drug companies give samples to doctors, trying to get them to prescribe their products. That case in the examination room is filled with samples."

From my amateurish perspective, just that declaration opens up a lot of new possibilities about Claire's death. Did someone get into the medicine cabinet? Are some of the potions and drugs subtle, yet progressively deadly? And most alarming, could one of the doctors have been dispensing too many, or the wrong, medications?

"I had never seen Claire walk, but you've told me she was able to, though with some effort," I say to Meredith.

"In her apartment she walked, slowly but rather steadily. She suffered from diabetes, so the circulation in her legs was faulty. Outside, where she wasn't familiar with the locales, she would be in her wheelchair."

"Yes," Charlotte adds, "when we would go to New Hope, to

Wally's, we would park in a handicap zone, she would instruct me to leave the chair in the car and she would amble the few steps into the café with me holding onto her arm. She was a rather proud person and hated to be waited on. The blindness was an insult."

"Do either of you know if there are any outspoken homophobes living in the Village?" I ask.

Charlotte shrugs and says, "These are old people and the new openness about sexual preference is radical for many of them. I would guess that some are homophobic, yet, for similar reasons gays choose to remain in the closet, a lot of these senior citizens clam up about their prejudices. They don't immediately know the viewpoint of the other person, and don't want to seem antiquated or ignorant."

"Unexpressed prejudice," I say softly. "That is a recipe for frustration—and maybe a spill-over into ugly behavior."

"Possibly," Charlotte says, her inside information a lot more formidable than mine, "but there are a dozen alternatives here. Claire sometimes had regular visitors from the outside, people who were friendly with her and would come for coffee or tea. And the relatives of some of the residents knew her as well, and might have had access. All that, along with the possibility of prescription overdoses, either accidental or purposeful."

"*Purposeful*," Meredith says, her face drawn up in a scowl—not scowl-like enough as I saw her, to mar her natural beauty.

"Oh, I don't know," Charlotte replies at once. "It's only an off-hand comment about possibilities. Aside from Drs. Doolittle and Overstreet, there is Dr. Segal, who may have seen Claire once or twice, and also the couple of nurses in the clinic. Why omit anyone when we're scrabbling for clues?"

"Hey, Sis, how did you get so clever?"

"I'm not. But I am detailed and picky."

"When can we follow up on the list of medicines Grandmother was taking?" Meredith asks.

"I'll speak with Oscar tomorrow, show him what we have. He'll have his own records of prescriptions he's filled." She pauses, looks at both Meredith and me, and says, "Why don't the two of you disappear somewhere? Go into Langhorne or Newtown. They're only ten minutes away, and you can see a movie or go to the park or…whatever."

My sister, is she looking out for me, or am I being too self-centered? She may be looking out for both of us.

Meredith appears nonplussed, stares out the window for a moment, and says, "Sure, why not."

Damn, she certainly has another agenda going on. I wonder if she will be willing to share it with me.

Charlotte gives us both a hug and pats me on the back. "We'll get to the bottom of all this."

"But," I reply, "be careful. If there's a crazed killer out there, I don't want you to be taking risks."

She smiles. "To live is a risk."

6

WE SIT ON a green bench, quietly watching the flow of the Delaware, from left to right, a wide river at this point, with an occasional sandbar in the stream, and one tiny island maybe fifteen by twenty feet, holding scrub brush and a small, twisted tree.

Charlotte told me about the re-enactment every Christmastime, of Washington crossing the icy Delaware to attack the unsuspecting Hessians, a likely turning point in the American Revolutionary War. She told it to me with a repugnant look, as she said, "The 1976 event was supposed to be the grandest, the two-hundredth anniversary of the Crossing, only it was fouled by the overhead presence of helicopters."

Sitting in the little town of Washington's Crossing, I can imagine the towering figure of big George, standing in his skiff, showing his courage to his followers.

Meredith looks forlorn, and I am tempted to confront her despondency with straightforward questions, but realize that would be invading her privacy.

As so often happens with me, when I am aware of something, but choose to wait, the issue confronts itself. She breaks the silence with a soft but steady torrent of words.

"We've known each other a couple of years, and there is much about me you don't know. It's not as if I'm deliberately trying to be secretive, but I've had so much going on, emotionally, that I thought it better to let it be. I know you are a dear man, and I can imagine how frustrating it must be for you to be on the outside, looking in."

I manage to say, not altogether truthfully, "That's okay, Meredith. Secrets are part of all of us. I've never wanted to pry. I…uh, have my secrets, too."

She seems to ignore my pathetic little reply, and goes on. "You see, there was this fellow."

Ah, a fellow. I knew it! Here it comes, the kiss-off, the "I like you, but…" scenario, the "You're a good *friend*…" rationale. Not sure I want to hear it. The river becomes a tumultuous flow, its current noisy, competing for my attention, a distraction. Well, not really, I am glued to her face, an addict to her voice.

"His name was Ted. Theodore, actually. He was a writer, not famous, but talented. Had two novels published, neither a bestseller, but was learning his trade, and was convinced the next one would be his magnum opus. I told him he was a mix between Hemingway and Steinbeck, economical in words, yet focused on social themes. He would laugh at me and tell me I was grandiose."

I am beginning to feel annoyed. So, she had a romance with some big-shot author, and kept it from me. What's the point? Where is all this going?

"Paradoxically, he was a surfer, aesthetic and cultured on the one hand, and a hippy on the other. I was charmed by the contrasts, seduced by his vagaries, his seemingly incompatible interests. I'm not sure what pulled him to me; I mean I'm not all that talented, and I think of myself as rather uncomplicated."

"Oh, Meredith, you underestimate yourself. You are a deep person, smart and insightful, and beautiful inside and out." Saying this is my biggest risk ever with her.

"You're my friend, and of course you will see me in a positive way. But I don't think Ted viewed me the way you describe. Frankly, as I look back on it, I think he saw me—and I feel crude saying this—as a good lay!"

Hearing her say this, shamefully I admit, brings on a surge of passion in me. Nothing wrong with being a good lay, but Meredith is a hell of a lot more than that.

"Not sure what you say is crude," I reply, "but if he didn't see the elegant aspects of you, he didn't deserve you."

"Well, see, I looked at it that way too, but I was…hooked on him." She looks at me apologetically and continues. "I was in love with him. Drastically. Stupidly."

"I notice," I say, "that this whole time you have been saying 'was.' Tell me what happened, what the status is." I'm not really sure I want to hear it, but I can't stand the ambiguity.

She covers her face with her hand, seems to shiver, looks up and about at the woods across the river on the Jersey side, at the lapping water just below us. What she says first is escape, a retreat from the tension, relief from the personal stress.

"The river is amazing, so eternal, so carefree."

I wait, testing again my pattern of trying to be patient.

"He..." she starts, but stops abruptly.

"Look," I say, trying my best to be tender, "if this is too hard for you..."

"No," she says at once. "I want to tell you. I've been holding onto it for too long. Claire was the only person in the world who knew. She was my comfort, and now she's gone."

"It seems to me, you and Claire were mutual comforts. She had her secrets and you had yours."

She shakes her head, stares hard at the water, and says in a whisper. "Ted...drowned."

In the next few minutes, she lays out for me a horror story about her boyfriend surfing on a stormy day, with surging waves and tricky currents. He collided with another surfer in a freak accident when a wave that seemed to have a mind of its own crossed to the side, crushing the two surfers together. The other fellow was hurt but managed to get to the sand; Ted, apparently unconscious, went under and was... lost.

"I didn't find out about it for two days. We weren't married and no one thought to contact me. When he didn't call, I got worried and contacted a mutual friend, a good buddy of his, and he told me on the phone. I think I trashed my apartment."

"Meredith, I'm so sorry. That's terrible—and the way you found out."

"It happened over a year ago, and I'm still not over it. Ted was rare, in many ways a genius, but volatile and often unpredictable, maybe, in the long run, not right for me, but it felt right, and I felt devastated."

Now, what do I do with this? Some hidden part of me feels a sense of relief that this amazing woman is not connected to some other man, yet her grief is a blanket over everything in her life. I have seen her mood, been repelled by her distance, and it would be fool-hardy to presume anything about her and me.

She continues. "Isn't there supposed to be a time-limit on mourning? I mean after a year or so, aren't we supposed to get on with our lives?"

"I don't know of any guidelines on getting over grief. For some people it can be months, for others, years, and probably with some, never. They spend the rest of their days in sorrow."

For the first time in this entire exchange, she looks at me, in-tensely, as if searching for the essence of my last words. I'm aware of a man and a woman in a small skiff navigating the waters near the Jersey shore, laughing playfully, a vivid contrast with the mood on our little bench.

Meredith says, "That's sick, isn't it, to carry on for over a year or more? Ted is gone. I know that, so why can't I put him away?"

I hate sounding like the wise old man, but I say, "Grief is per-sonal. There is no yardstick. You'll be over it when you're over it."

Her hand is on her mouth as she stares out across the river. At last she nods and says in a soft voice, "You're very sweet. I do appre-ciate you."

It hits me in that moment that, along with the loss of her Theo-dore, she also has just suffered the loss of her dear grandmother, pos-sibly as a result of treachery. Those burdens must be tremendous.

The carefree couple in the boat (who knows if they are truly care-free?) have cruised around the slight bend in the river and are out of sight. Damn, but it is so true that all relationships carry burdens, un-known from a distance, and sometimes unknown even up close!

"Dear Meredith," I say, looking intensely back at her, "I love who you are, with all your history and baggage and pain. Nobody knows how long a heart will beat or lungs dole out oxygen. For me, it means to live it up. Enjoy moments. Cherish all this: the river, the November chill, the sapphire sky. I hope you find your own kind of peace, and soon."

Joy, ecstasy, bliss! She leans over and kisses me, only on the cheek, true, then reaches around and hugs me, hard and long.

7

CHARLOTTE PHONES me at the Blue Dolphin. After that riverside revelation, Meredith said she needed to be alone and drove me back to my motel. I read for two hours, ate a tuna sandwich at the motel coffee shop, and was asleep by ten o'clock. Emotional exhaustion is far more overwhelming than physical; I slept for ten hours.

"It's after nine o'clock. Are you up and around?" Charlotte asks.

"Yep. Showered, shaved, made awful coffee in my room, and am steamed up for a busy day." I know there is less than a week left on my vacation, and I'll be returning to California shortly. That alone weighs on me like a too-heavy barbell, especially since it means I'll be saying goodbye again to Meredith, maybe for months or even a year.

"My pal, Oscar, opens his pharmacy at nine each morning. I wonder if you'd like to accompany me when I take him Claire's prescription list?"

"It's a bit too far for me to walk."

"Silly me, of course. I'll pick you up."

She is at my motel in fifteen minutes and we head to a little shopping mall a few blocks from Bigelow Village.

"I've been thinking," Charlotte says in the car, "about Meredith. Poor girl has lost a true companion, and we do not quite honor her position in all this. I believe my pursuit of a perpetrator, suspicious as I am, may prolong her sense of loss. I wonder how wise all that is."

"It cuts both ways," I say. "She is suffering from Claire's death, of course, but she is also incensed that anyone would want to…well there is no other word but, *murder* her lovely grandmother. I think she needs closure, and uncovering the architect of this ugly deed would give it to her."

"Good point," Charlotte says as she maneuvers into a parking spot near a two-story brownstone building with a darkly tinted glass front. "Oscar's pharmacy is in here. When residents of Bigelow need prescriptions filled, the Village driver will shuttle them here."

There is an oversized window and a counter, standard for pharmacies, and along the walls a dozen drug varieties advertised as helpful for depression, anxiety, prostate issues, restless legs, insomnia, and a myriad other ailments. I am reminded of how drug-saturated our culture is, and why children seem to slide so easily into using them; who decides which ones are the good ones?

The proprietor stands inside and greets us.

"Oscar here?" Charlotte asks the youngish man, dressed all in white.

"In back. Lots of prescriptions to mix up."

"Would you tell him, please, that Charlotte Smart is here, from Bigelow Village."

It takes three minutes and a grinning fellow turns a corner and appears at the counter. He leans over, as does Charlotte, and he kisses her cheek.

"Not the time of the month for your medicines," Oscar says. "You must be on a mission." He is tall and thin, not too far removed from a replica of the Scarecrow in The Wizard of Oz, and I imagine that he admirably adheres to all the vitamin and mineral and omega-3 food choices that bombard the public these days. He, also, is clad all in white.

"How did you get so smart, Double O? You must see two thousand customers a week, and here you are remembering my dates."

"Ah, Charlotte," he says, his lower lip thrust upward, "you are special, you know. Can't forget the special ones."

"This is my brother, Greg, visiting from California."

He thrusts out a thin hand, mostly bone, yet grips mine with surprising strength. "A pleasure to meet you, Greg."

"Likewise," I say, and can't help but feel his authenticity as well as his fondness for my sister.

"So, tell me your mission," he says abruptly to Charlotte, the niceties over.

"See this? You remember Claire Hazelton, my friend who

passed, over a week ago? I have some question about the medications she was taking. I want you to tell me about this list, what is compatible with what, and what might be toxic if over-dosed."

"Aha," he says, eyes gleaming as if getting into a meaty investigation will infuse excitement into his back-room tedium.

We are silent for a full two minutes as his trained eye peruses the list of prescribed medicines and supplements the doctors gave Claire.

At last he says, "Mission accomplished. We have Hazelton's record, but normally don't look for patterns. This Dr. Overstreet loves to prescribe painkillers and ends up being a pain in the ass. I've had conversations with him about this, but he has a supercilious attitude about the older folks at Bigelow. Anything they complain about, he prescribes a steroid. Steroids are cumulative. A single one can relieve hurt and inflammation, but combine them or mix in too many, and you have a formula for hypoxia, which is a deficiency of oxygen reaching the body tissues. If the blood has insufficient oxygenation, it can lead to dizziness and eventually a brain deficit."

I listen to this, and my untutored mind leaps to a conclusion, that Claire was probably not deliberately killed, but was erroneously stuffed with the wrong medicines by a careless doctor.

My sister is, I guess, less gullible than I, because she says, "Yet, such a prescriptive overdose may or may not lead to collapse, am I right? I mean, people do correct the condition when they feel burdened."

"Oh, yes. Well, you know, steroids, by themselves, are supposed to increase strength and bulk up the body. Witness all those dumb athletes who got into trouble. But, over the years, the build-up can trigger side effects. I don't know about Claire Hazelton, but she was a big woman, and I'd be willing to bet her size was a product of all those steroids Overstreet was stipulating."

"Excuse me, Oscar, but we are of the opinion that Ms. Hazelton may have been the victim of foul play. Your testimony here seems to indict Overstreet as a careless doctor, yet I don't catch any deliberate intent to harm."

"Charlotte, Overstreet is a pompous, self-congratulating ass. None of my clerks likes him. And that's without any of them, except me, having personally met the man. He's a biased medical fool, but he isn't a killer. No, I wouldn't say he did anything deliberate."

"So," I insert, "do you have any thoughts about what might have been the cause of Ms. Hazelton's demise?"

"Selenium."

"Say again?" Charlotte asks.

"Selenium is a supplement that mixes with vitamin E to fight oxidation. It exists in nature, and is often taken as a supplement in pill form. We know, however, that too much selenium is toxic."

"Go on," Charlotte says.

"Claire Hazelton would pick up a plastic container of selenium—no prescription needed—every couple of weeks. Now, it says on the bottle, serving size one pill, which is one or two hundred micrograms. She was blind, of course, and it made it a challenge to pick up the correct container and follow the directions. The steroids were sometimes taken three at a time, but the selenium needed to be limited to one. Who knows if she grabbed the wrong bottle?"

"There were no bottles or plastic containers of any kind next to her body when she was found," Charlotte says.

"Well, the result is not instantaneous. She could have overdosed and then put the bottles away, only to pass out several minutes later."

"Or," Charlotte says, almost as if talking to herself, "someone who was supposedly helping her with her selections might have..." She lets the sentence hang in the air.

Oscar catches Charlotte's implication and adds, "A study was done on five Chinese patients who exhibited overt signs of selenosis, and it was found they had eaten corn grown in selenium-rich stony shale. A selenium dose of as small as five milligrams a day can be lethal for many humans."

"But, why take it at all?" I ask.

"Because it is an essential trace element, that comes from nuts, cereals, meat, fish, and eggs, and there are numerous studies that show when combined with a couple hundred units of vitamin E per day, it can be a potent antioxidant—meaning a tumor inhibitor."

"So," Charlotte says, "it is a necessary element in its proper dosage, but deadly when overdone."

"You got it."

"Thank you, Oscar. The steroids are the doctor's excess but the selenium is either an unfortunate error, or some miscreant's deliberate sabotage of a woman who was ultra-vulnerable."

"Got to get back in my cave," Oscar says. "If you need anything else from me, let me know."

"You are a sweetheart," Charlotte says.

As we exit the glass-fronted building, she says to me. "I've known Claire all these years. Blind as she was, she never made errors like that. Her medications, as with everything else in her living space, were marked, either with raised letters, or with attached indicators. She was fastidious about her environmental needs."

I think those words over for a minute or two, and, as we drive away, I reflect, "It becomes a slippery task of trying to figure out who wanted to do her in, and how he or she did it."

Charlotte takes her eyes off the road for a moment and smiles at me. "We need to gain access to Claire's room. Those pill bottles are still in there, and they may speak to us in the most illuminating ways."

8

DAYS IN THE FALL are short, and the afternoon light seems prematurely subverted by the encroaching darkness. If it had a voice, the brightness might complain: *Unfair to take me away before I have filled up people's lives with light.* Just my romantic non sequitur as I think about us driving toward Meredith.

We fill Meredith in on what Oscar said, and though it takes some doing to get permission, as the last rays of sunlight careen through the leafless maples outside her window, Charlotte returns to her apartment with the key to Claire's.

The long halls that connect the wings of the Village are illuminated by bulbs in the shape of little torches, set high up on the walls. Even with the lighting, in the twilight, the tunnels seem eerie and ominous. I doubt I would perceive it so if we were not pursuing some culprit, someone with the capacity for evil. I am not usually morose, or even suspicious.

It often surprises me when things work out as planned. I recall setting up a rendezvous with a friend in London, on a corner near his bed-and-breakfast place. I told him my flight number, he told me how far his spot was from Heathrow, and we set the time for meeting. I came up, out of the underground, and there he was, grinning, with his hand out. Bowled me over that there were no glitches in our arrangements. Perhaps I am a bit suspicious, after all, at least of serendipity.

This scheme also goes as planned. Charlotte slips the key she was given into the lock in Claire's door, saying, "I told them she was my best friend, and her granddaughter and I needed to go over her things."

Voila! It works. The door opens.

"They'll be coming in soon to clean out her quarters so they can lease them out to someone else. It's a business, you know."

"Yes," Meredith says. "They informed me that if there's anything I want, it needs to be removed by next Saturday. Whatever's left behind will either be throw away or donated to charity."

"A life dwindles down to things," I say. "Possessions identify us. We are what we own."

"True," Charlotte says, "and if one of our residents is alone in the world, without family, her entire existence here is erased inside of a month."

The thought of Charlotte being so erased hits me in the chest. Charlotte is my dear sister; her life being erased is something I vow to myself I will not allow. Charlotte enters with her usual confidence. The flat looks as if nothing catastrophic has happened, everything in place, braille books on a coffee table, a music system along a far wall, and a television prominent, though the viewing was obviously for her visitors. The kitchen is neat and clean, no dishes anywhere, even in the drainer—order one might expect in a four-star restaurant, ready for inspection.

Charlotte heads at once for the bathroom. Since there was no indication of a crime, there are no yellow police streamers, and no markings where Claire's body was discovered.

I am stunned at what Charlotte does next. From a pocket in the apron-like blouse she is wearing, she pulls out a pair of thin rubber gloves and slips them on.

"I saw it on television," she says, looking chagrined at our stares.

"Hey, go for it," I say.

Meredith says, "Why do I feel as if you always know the right thing to do?"

"Because Charlotte does," I reply.

"Go easy on the praise," Charlotte says. "I'm as amateurish as the two of you. I try to think ahead, that's all. With people who break the law, one must be ahead of them."

"Can't imagine anyone getting the jump on you, Sis," and there is pride in my voice.

"Well," she says, and she is smiling at me, "let's see what we come up with."

The medicine cabinet is standard, though once opened I can see that the shelves actually have braille on them as an aide for a blind person. Everything seems to have been structured to keep Claire from making errors.

Carefully, one by one, Charlotte lifts each item from its shelf, examines its label, and sets it on the lid of the back of the toilet. In a few moments there are twenty small containers side by side. My sister seems to pause, then peers down acutely at her collection, perusing them with what seems to me a practiced eye.

As if in deliberate contradiction, she says, "I don't know what I'm looking for."

Meredith and I glance at each other, and Meredith says, almost incredulously, "You don't?"

"Well," comes the reply, "the usual labels on medications have been replaced by braille figures so Claire would know what capsules she was taking." She pauses, and then adds, "What it means is that if someone had offered to help her and instead fed her the toxic pills, that person would have needed to know what was in each container, or understand braille."

Brilliant! My big sis is indeed an amazing sleuth.

"Who would have changed the labels to braille?" Meredith asks.

"There is a center on blindness that cooperates with our facility, since so many of our residents have failing eyesight. It's called Vision-Aide. I'm sure Claire was serviced by them, so that may need to be our next stop."

Again, as if she knows exactly what to do, Charlotte slides all the bottles into a plastic bag, also dug out from her apron pocket.

"We'll take these with us. At some point, the local gendarmes need to get involved. These containers may produce prints or other leads."

As we leave Claire's apartment, Charlotte says, "It might be helpful to count the remaining pills in each bottle and match their number with the dates Oscar has for their purchase."

Since it is evening, and too late to follow up with Vision-Aide, we return to Charlotte's apartment, and she offers us glasses of what she pleasingly describes as "One of those wonderful California wines."

It is not until we are seated in sort of a triangle facing the television, that Meredith says, "What's that slip of paper on the carpet?"

We had stepped right over it, but there, only a few inches in from the door, is a folded sheet of amber-colored paper.

"Hmm," Charlotte says, and goes to retrieve it. She sits back down, reads the note, and holds it up for the two of us to see.

In cut-out letters, taken from what appears to be newspaper print, we see:

YOU ARE INTERFERING.
YOU ARE CAUSING TROUBLE.
BACK OFF.

"Uh-oh," I say.

"Well," Meredith says, "that erases any doubt about accidental overdoses."

Charlotte looks thoughtful, and at last says, "We need to think clearly about two things: whom are we threatening, and what access does that person have to these surroundings?"

"Your apartment is only a few steps from the elevator, so someone could have slipped the paper under your door without much fuss. But still, the person had to know which your place is."

"More than that," Charlotte responds. "She or he would also have to know what we've been up to. So, we may be talking about a person we've been in touch with the last few days."

My mind begins to race over all the folks, both in and out of the Village, whom we'd encountered, their reactions and interest in our search. But besides all that, the implication behind the letter sends a chill up my spine.

"Charlotte," I say, "this is a clear threat to you. Subtle as Claire's death may have been, there is no guarantee that the perpetrator will be as subtle next time."

I catch a fleeting look of fear in Charlotte's eyes, and then a quick dismissal as she says, "At my age, threats aren't all that fierce." She smiles wanly. "I'll have to watch what I eat in the dining room."

"What about the police?" I ask. "Isn't this enough proof that something nasty is going on? Shouldn't we bring them in on it?"

"I agree," Meredith says. "Grandmother was deliberately killed, the killer is demented and could be dangerous, and the authorities need to be consulted."

"Salud!" Charlotte says, and raises her wine glass. "The wine comes first."

9

THE NEXT DAY, just after lunch as we reconvened in Charlotte's apartment, there is a knock at the door, and when Charlotte opens it a tall man steps through.

"Augustus Hartunian, at your service, though friends all call me Augie," he says. "Strange mix of names, I know, but my father was Armenian and my mother Greek. My name is a piece of both. How can I help?"

"I'm Charlotte Smart. And this is my brother, Greg, and the victim's granddaughter, Meredith. We need your assistance in what we now know is a dreadful matter, detective."

"Hartunian," I insert, "I know a Hartunian out in Los Angeles. He's a detective, too. A friend of mine was on the fringes of a case he helped solve."

"Yeah, he's my uncle, my dad's older brother, Carl. My role model and a very successful detective, a guy with surprising heart for victims and suspects. Likes the big city crime stuff; I like the country crime better. But wait, did you say there was a victim?"

Country crime, odd way to put it, I think, but I remain silent as Meredith says, "Well, officer, I don't like any crime, and especially when it involves my grandmother. She was murdered, and we need to find out why and by whom."

"Murdered? You have a murder here?"

"We do, Detective Hartunian," Charlotte says, that intense gleam in her eye flashing as she produces the note and other bits of what we all think of as incontrovertible evidence.

Before handing it over, she takes five minutes to give Hartunian the background on Claire, her life–though not every detail–and her sudden death.

"Whooey," the detective says. "We haven't had a murder around these parts in years. Now, I suppose we ought to find out if she really was murdered, and if so, who might have resented her and for what reasons. I mean, after all, an elderly person can hardly be thought of as a serious threat."

Hartunian shows no outward signs of being a policeman, no badge on his lapel, no trench coat–though that may be my generalization–and no obvious bulges in his jacket pockets. He is tall and dark, with bushy eyebrows and light grey eyes; his hair is trimmed short, without a part, and still brown, but with a bare touch of white in the sideburns.

Charlotte says, "Not to contradict you, detective, but threat is an internal experience, and we never know who might be sensing it."

"Right, right, ma'am," he replies, seeming not to want to be at odds with any of us.

"She had two things that might have triggered anger," Meredith says, "the fact that she was a lesbian, and her belief system, which was atheist."

Hartunian looks thoughtful, and says, "Wouldn't think those things would drive a person to murder." He sees our very serious faces, and adds, "Of course, you never know."

"Along with that," I say, "she had a history of confronting folks; granted it was when she was living in California, and granted it was several years ago. So, at one time, she seemed to have enemies."

"Enemies," Hartunian says, stroking his chin thoughtfully.

To me, he seems too diffident to be a cop, backing off of any sort of disagreement, hardly an incisive thinker. But now he says something that alters my perception.

"I'll take that bag of medications to our lab. We're kind of a hick operation here, but we do have one excellent forensics person to test for prints and the contents of each container. Could be that some bottles got switched, or maybe some pills substituted for others. In the meantime, this note is a genuine threat, and I don't want anyone else getting hurt. So, to stay out of trouble is the order of the day, and that means no private investigations. No sleuthing around."

"Oh, we're not foolish enough to try to catch the bad guy by ourselves," Charlotte says.

I'm not sure he catches the subtle sarcasm in her voice, but I know when my sister is putting someone on. The three of accompany the detective to the parking lot.

As he leaves the complex, Detective Hartunian says, as if tossing off something trivial, "Murder is an act of desperation, when every other remedy seems pointless." And with that he nods to us and is gone.

He may have thought his comment was cryptic and mysterious, but Charlotte's head turns to the side as softly she says, "Yes, and we must now focus in on who could be so desperate."

—

"I wish to correct something I said earlier," Charlotte tells us. We are in Meredith's car, on our way to Vision-Aide. "It does not necessarily have to be someone we spoke with or saw in—what did Hartunian call it—our sleuthing around?"

"Oh?" Meredith replies, her eyes peering ahead on a day of rain and slick roads.

"You see, the Village is a cornucopia for gossip. One person knows something, everyone knows it."

"Ah," I say, "a person we either questioned, or told information to, could have likely told others."

"Not likely; certainly," Charlotte says.

"That broadens the field," Meredith says. "A hell of a lot more suspects if the whole retirement complex knows about us."

She steers her car up a slight grade and over a small bridge spanning a creek that I can see is busy with too much water from the rainfall. In my hometown, we get virtually no rain until December, and then none again after April. These November showers are rather pleasant for me, though I can see how it makes Meredith work harder at the wheel.

"Considering the note," Charlotte puts in, her eyes studying the road ahead, as if she were driving, "it still means that the person has to know where I live and how to maneuver the halls in Bigelow Village."

"Yes," I say. "So perhaps that eliminates those we contacted away from the complex."

"Hmm," Charlotte ponders, "I don't think so. We have no way

of knowing who has visited in the past, and which, if any, outsiders were Claire's friends. I knew her pretty well, but I live in a different hallway on the second floor. She was downstairs and closer to the dining hall and the front desk. In fact, because of her blindness, she was in a section where more intensive care took place. In her apartment is a buzzer that brings help within a couple of minutes."

"So, an outsider could have been coming to see her, perhaps a friend, or at least someone she knew, and that person might have been *helping* her…with the medications," I say, as if to myself.

"Ah," Charlotte says, again gently contradicting, "but you see, the helper need not have been the murderer. The pill bottles might have been contaminated, and the friend, not knowing that, could have offered to help, when in reality, he or she was poisoning Claire."

"Diabolical!" I say loudly.

"But then the friend is an unwitting accomplice," Meredith says.

"Well, I doubt that the officials would look at it that way. But, as you can see, that complicates matters."

We have rolled into a small town and Meredith steers to the right and then turns sharply into the parking lot of a three-story building. The lot is nearly full since it services the Vision-Aide folks, a shoe store, a deli, a mom and pop clothing store, and a hamburger hut attached to the side of the larger building. It is later in the morning, and most who are going to work are already there. Few other cars seem to be moving about.

As we scurry in the rain to the eaves of the office building, I realize that in six days, I will return to California. If I hope to be in on any resolution of this horrible event, it will have to be in that span of time. Damn, even Sherlock Holmes sometimes took a few weeks to solve a murder. Well, perhaps Charlotte–or Detective Hartunian–can perform a miracle and crack the case in record time.

Why none of us thought to bring an umbrella or two, I don't know, so we are pretty wet when we open the heavy glass door to the Vision-Aide building. Meredith seems annoyed by it, Charlotte unfazed, and I—well, I'm actually enjoying the rare feeling. We pass a hall mirror and I notice my face wet and flushed, a bead of water hanging like a dewdrop from my nose.

The interior door is also glass and we can see through it a busy office with four employees on computers or phones. The one closest to the door, a middle-aged woman with sunny yellow hair, looks up, smiles, and says, "Hello there; may I help you?"

"We're on the board at Bigelow Village," Charlotte lies, "and are following up on the tragic death of one of our residents, Claire Hazelton. She was blind, and you folks were servicing her."

"Oh," the woman says in a husky voice. "One minute, please. Helen handles the Bigelow accounts." She presses a small white button on her desk and a tall woman enters from around a corner in the interior. She has a smile–looks theatrical to me–plastered on her face, and strides toward us briskly.

"Helen Cumberland. How may I help you?"

I notice a large, silver cross on a chain around her neck, resting on her bare chest, revealing cleavage and a plentiful bosom. I have often wondered about women who flaunt their religious affiliation at the same time they flaunt their sexuality. Nothing basically wrong about that, but it does seem, to my naïve way of seeing things, like a contradiction. Helen Cumberland is wearing gloves, the same, thin, rubber variety that Charlotte wore when she inspected the pill bottles.

Charlotte says, "The Board at Bigelow Village has asked us to follow up on the death of Claire Hazelton, one of your customers. We understand you were servicing her account."

"Yes," Ms. Cumberland says, pointing to a small circle of soft chairs in the waiting area. "Please sit down."

She does not seem interested in our names and Charlotte does not volunteer them. Helen Cumberland is nearly six-feet tall, an imposing figure, yet she wears a muted beige suit, very business-like–in fact everything about her is business-like, except, I ponder, her low-cut top. Though perhaps I am wrong, since I am not in business per se. Displaying one's skin may be a perfectly acceptable business gesture, designed, possibly, to attract potential clients.

"What we are interested in learning," Charlotte says in a matter-of-fact tone, "is how Ms. Hazelton's prescription labels were turned into braille labels. There is some concern that the labels of her pill containers did not match the contents of the bottles. We just want to tidy up all our information on her death."

"We service dozens of vision-impaired clients, mostly elderly, every week," Ms. Cumberland says. "Quite a few are at Bigelow. They get their prescriptions from the pharmacy, then approach us to make braille labels to cover the standard written labels. I monitored Ms. Hazelton's account along with the others for Bigelow."

"Ah," Charlotte says, "and did you do that here at your offices, or did you visit her quarters in the Village?"

"Our clients usually stop in once a month, after getting new meds, and wait–right here, actually–while we alter their labels. We have special equipment, a braille typewriter, and it only takes twenty minutes to type up a dozen labels. In Ms. Hazelton's case, I did visit her apartment twice over the past year, since she called to tell us that she did not have transportation."

"So," Meredith asks, "you have a portable braille typewriter?"

"Oh yes. Though a bit heavy, it is quite compact and easy to use. When we agree to make a home visit it is almost always for more than one client. In Ms. Hazelton's case, at least the last time we did it, there were two others we serviced at the same visit."

"Which was when?" Charlotte asks.

"Let me see.... I think it was...twelve days ago. Yes, I'm sure it was, because I had an appointment with my doctor, listed in my schedule book for that same day." She pauses, and adds, "I suffer from fibromyalgia."

Cumberland smiles as if to elicit sympathy, though the only re-action is from Charlotte who says, "Sorry to hear that. I'm sure you are on a regimen of pills and medicines yourself for that affliction."

"Unfortunately, yes. It is an illness that causes fatigue and cuts into sleep. I take a combination of meds, carefully monitored, of course."

"Getting back to Ms. Hazelton," I say, "when you visited her twelve days ago, did she seem healthy to you? No unusual symp-toms?"

"Well, I didn't know her all that well, but she seemed as she al-ways seemed. Aside from her blindness, she was a sturdy woman–or so I thought. Of course, God works in mysterious ways, and we never know when we will be summoned."

"Yes," Meredith says, "and her death was a surprise. She was pretty vigorous when I last saw her, which was maybe two weeks ago."

"I wasn't aware the board actually visited the clients at Bigelow. That's very thorough."

"So, you covered the pharmacy labels with braille labels at that time. Did you also administer any doses to her?" Charlotte asks.

"No, of course not. That is not part of our work. Our job is to help the client to help herself. I was there around ten in the morning, and I would imagine she had already taken her prescribed daily doses by then."

"One other question, Ms. Cumberland," Charlotte says softly, but with a bite in her voice, as if asserting 'and I expect an answer.' "Do you have any recollection at all of what the labels on Claire Hazelton's pill containers read?"

"Oh my, no. We have far too many requests for me to keep them in my mind. However, our braille writers not only produce the labels, but keep a record of what was printed out. I can retrieve that information for you, if you like."

"That would be nice. Can you do it now? We'll be happy to wait." Ms. Cumberland rises—she looks even taller—and moves back into the interior of her offices. When she is gone, Charlotte says, "Impressive woman. Fills up a room. But I get a clear sense of resentment coming from her."

"Resentment?" Meredith asks.

"You catch her religious references? She must have known that Claire had none. Resentment. Who knows what resentment can lead to?"

"Damn," I mutter, "just when I think I know who might have wanted to hurt Claire, someone else leaps out in front."

"My grandmother was a sweet woman, but with strong beliefs. I can see where she could have alienated certain groups or individuals with opposite strong beliefs."

"Certainly," Charlotte says, "and she could have alienated some folks over things other than beliefs. Don't forget about the police harassment issues when she was younger; some people never forget. And also remember her partner, with whom she broke up—resentment can certainly be a byproduct of rejection."

Charlotte's ruminations make my head spin. They introduce all sorts of possibilities. Motives are personal and deep, and nobody from the outside can be sure of what stirs a person from the inside.

Ms. Cumberland strides around the back desk and heads toward us, her right arm extended. When she arrives she says tersely, "Here. This is a record of what we printed out from the last visit. Those labels are what ought to be on the bottles."

"Thank you," Charlotte says graciously. "You have been very helpful."

"Of course; it is my pleasure." Almost as an afterthought, and certainly spoken with disregard for the consequences, Helen Cumberland turns to move back to her workplace. "Believers and disbelievers alike are taken," she says imperiously. "The difference is where they go."

10

IT IS STILL raining, a special East Coast November kind of cold rain, as we drive away from Vision-Aide. Charlotte, seated in the front passenger seat, says, in an elevated tone to override the rainfall and the windshield wipers, "Another of our residents—you met her, Freda, the outspoken one—suffers from fibromyalgia. I researched it online when she told me. That was a few months ago, but I remembered a good deal of it."

"Like what?" I ask, leaning forward from the back seat as much as the seatbelt will allow.

"Fibromyalgia is an incurable affliction that causes chronic pain. Because of all the medications that are tried on them, folks suffering from it are at particular risk to develop a rare but increasingly common condition called serotonin syndrome."

"Serotonin?" Meredith asks. "Isn't that the natural hormone produced in the brain to regulate a person's mood?"

"It's a chemical messenger," Charlotte says. "Folks with pain or depression often take prescribed drugs that help release serotonin into the bloodstream."

"So, what is this syndrome?" I ask.

"Serotonin syndrome appears to result from combining two or more drugs designed to release the hormone, or when a medication is used that inhibits the liver's ability to cleanse the bloodstream. When the bloodstream can't be cleansed, excess serotonin builds up."

"Then what?" Meredith asks. "Too much serotonin can be dangerous?"

Charlotte takes a deep breath and says, "This adds one other possibility to Claire's death, and we really do need to get an autopsy report. Yes, symptoms of serotonin syndrome often appear when one additional medication is added to a person's regimen, causing an overload. It can result in dizziness, disorientation, sweating, or shivering. It can become severe, and can bring on complications like high blood pressure, loss of consciousness, or stroke. It can lead to death."

"Jesus!" I say. "This Cumberland woman would know all about that. And we have her own admission that she was with Claire just days before Claire's death."

"We do, but we do not know if she is snooty or indecent, or that she did anything malicious to Claire. At this point, it is simply one other option to consider."

"Let's not forget," Meredith says, "that Freda would also know all about the syndrome. Kind of puts her on the hook as well."

Charlotte smiles. "I know Freda pretty well, and I wouldn't put anything past her. She marches to a different drummer, likes to think she has her own value system, and can do whatever she pleases."

"Freedom." I say. "Freedom for Freda!"

"True," Charlotte responds. "But freedom has an awesome twin: responsibility."

There is silence in the car, the dominant sound is the relentless cadence of the windshield wipers, like an overwrought pulsebeat. I like it, but Meredith continues to labor at the wheel, and is thankfully cautious and slow paced.

At last she says, "I can't believe Grandmother is dead. In her way, she was more alive than people half her age."

In the momentary quiet that follows, the three of us seem deep in thought. Charlotte then says, "It kind of attacks the smugness so many of us get about our lives. The most learned and the most famous all face the remorseless indifference of death."

—

In Charlotte's apartment, her answering machine is blinking red. We listen: "Hallo there, Ms. Smart. This is Detective Hartunian. Want you to know that in our preliminary check on the bottles, we found prints that, of course, belong to Ms. Hazelton, but also to Wally Burt.

Mr. Burt is in our system because a few years back he was arrested for blocking the street when a political dignitary he didn't like was in town. Doesn't tell us anything except that he touched those containers. Oh, and remember, don't do anything I wouldn't do. Ha ha! That's not right. Don't do anything you *shouldn't* do."

"Well," Charlotte says. "So, Wally visited Claire. And more than likely, he helped her by administering some of the pills. As Hartunian says, we cannot impose any intent on his actions, since it could all be naively done."

"It is remarkable to me that Claire never told me anything about Wally," Meredith says, a clear sense of insult in her voice. "A man whose café she regularly frequented with you, Charlotte, and who came to her apartment to help her."

"As I have said, I knew Claire as a very private person. I would guess that her life choices made her pull in for protection," Charlotte says, as she lays her damp overcoat onto an old-fashioned radiator along the window. "Here," she adds and reaches for our coats, "let me dry out yours as well. Nice rain, but it can give a chill."

—

We spend a few hours relaxing, reading, and drinking more tea, the rain a somber inhibitor of action. When the first slanting rays of sun begin to nibble at the windowpane, Charlotte says, "Okay, time to get moving. It's fun just hanging out with you two handsome people, but we have work to do."

Meredith smiles warmly at my sister. "You are quick with compliments," she says. "Who compliments you?"

"Oh, Greg does. Our last name is Smart, and he is always telling me how apropos my name is."

"He's right. You are, and crafty, too. What do you see as the next item on our agenda?"

"I think the three of us ought to pay a little visit to Dr. Lyle Overstreet. I checked the schedule and he is on duty today. His standard steroid prescriptions seem excessive to me, if not downright suspicious, and, as of this moment, we can't rule that out as a contributor to Claire's death."

"Ah," I say. "The plot thickens. Even the good doctor could be a suspect."

"I don't mean to imply that he sought Claire's demise, but he seems callous to the elderly folks here at Bigelow, and I would like to confront him with the possible consequences of his indifference."

We begin the trek down the long corridors, the outside sunlight now making them less eerie, and I reach to take Meredith's hand. She lets me.

The clinic area is nearly empty. I suppose, on a stormy day, a lot of folks settle in at home, though we do not have to go outside to reach the door labeled "Medical."

On the way, we encounter Freda, sitting in the small library, reading the *New York Times*. She sees us passing and issues a thumbs-up, but when we are out of her sight, Charlotte whispers, "Don't buy into that affirmation. She's the crafty one."

There is one window in the clinic unit, and through it I can see the trees in the garden of the Village, their naked limbs poking out and upward, looking gossamer and unworldly. The interior, by contrast, seems tidy and antiseptic, in fact markedly sterile.

A nurse greets Charlotte with a smile and a repeated nod. She seems stuck in that action, as if obsessively driven.

"Hello Penny," Charlotte says. "We don't have an appointment, but it is imperative that we see Dr. Overstreet." She hesitates and for emphasis adds, "It's about our dear friend, Claire, who passed last week."

"I'm sure he'll be happy to speak with you. He's with one of our older octogenarians, who is suffering from an ingrown toenail."

More than we need to know, I think. After all, medical issues are supposed to be confidential. Charlotte frowns.

We step back and sit in the small waiting area and Charlotte says to Meredith and me, "She's Overstreet's special nurse. Has the same attitude about the elderly as the doctor. *'They're just old folks. Privacy doesn't matter. They're almost dead, anyway.'*"

Her words stir me to thinking about the thin line between life and death. That, after all, is our language for categorizing a changeable thing into an inert thing. We are all composed of atoms, neurons, and electrons, recyclable and, in the end, recycled.

Creepy to think that way, but it helps me to realize how important it is to live fully each day.

Meredith catches my pensive mood and asks, "What are you pondering?"

I laugh and say, "The meaning of life."

A bulky man, unshaven and dressed in white, approaches us and greets Charlotte.

"What can I do for you, Charlotte?" He is not hostile, but neither is he amiable. He is all business, with an attitude of 'what sort of problem do I have to deal with now?'

"Dr. Overstreet, this is my friend, Meredith, and my brother, Greg. Meredith is Claire Hazelton's granddaughter. We are on an expedition."

"Oh. Tell me what sort? Seeking hidden treasure? Looking for a lost tribe?" He laughs at his own attempt at humor, which I find distasteful. Folks who think they are funny usually are not. He sours my mood.

"Let me get right to the point," Charlotte says, her manner in keeping with his. I can see she is not enamored of this man, and will, herself, be all business. "The police are involved in Claire's death. It is highly likely that it was not a natural event, but rather a crime, perpetrated by another."

His face scrunches up into wrinkles, his mouth open, eyes wide, hand on his chin. The words that come are deliberate and slow: "You are speaking of murder."

"I am."

There is a long pause. "How can I help you?" he asks.

"I am helping, informally collecting information, for Meredith and the officials," Charlotte says, coolly. "There are several possibilities. The detectives know that you have been prescribing steroids, and we have researched that a build-up in someone's body can be dangerous. We also know that she was taking selenium, and that an overdose could be toxic. Besides that, we are concerned that Claire might possibly have suffered from serotonin syndrome, a result of taking the wrong meds. We would appreciate any insight you can give us about any of these details."

He stares at Charlotte intensely, the impact of her words slowly, yet certainly, beginning to come through. That his actions might have been a factor in Ms. Hazelton's death must, as the great bard wrote, give him pause.

"Aha," he says, spins about, walks a few paces, and returns. Penny, some yards away, looks startled and apprehensive.

"Elderly patients are…flimsy," Overstreet says. "Steroids are like Ritalin, in that both give them energy and tone, without some of the side effects. And yes, if it is not monitored, it could cause illness—there are recorded cases of cancer with too much steroid consumption. But,

I gather that Ms. Hazelton did not die of cancer."

"You gather correctly, Doctor," I say.

He gives me a nasty look, and says, "Then the steroid thesis is probably faulty. As to selenium, it is not a prescriptive drug, and can be purchased over the counter. Directions are clear about usage. Though she was blind, I presume she knew how to identify her drugs."

"She had all her labels redone in braille. Her medicine cabinet was a splendid panoply of raised letters," Charlotte assures him.

"Serotonin syndrome results from varied combinations of meds that trigger too much serotonin into the bloodstream. And yes, I have read of strokes or seizures, and even death as a result. But, since she did not suffer from fibromyalgia, which is a common diagnosis for using serotonin-enhancing meds, I don't see how she would have an over-abundance in her system."

"Yes," Charlotte says. "But there is the possibility that labels were tampered with, and we are researching whether someone—the culprit, actually—planted serotonin-liberating drugs in her medicines."

Overstreet smiles, not a friendly smile, but an insider's smile, as if he knows more than anyone else. "There, you see. We diagnose and prescribe, and have little to do with whether elderly patients follow directions properly." He stops, and adds, "The whole thing could have been a dreadful accident. They get confused. They make mistakes."

"Grandmother," Meredith says, with as much venom in her voice as I have ever heard, "did not make such mistakes. Someone did this to her, and we are going to find out who!"

Overstreet is taken aback. I have seen how he has been ogling Meredith—he is, after all, youngish and likely on the prowl—and now, this lustrous woman puts out a broad yet pointed challenge to the world.

"Of course," he says, noticeably subdued. "Our records are open to the officials. There are no secrets. Now if there is nothing else, I need to get back to my patients."

I see no one else in the clinic, so I don't know which patients he means, but presume he needs to escape. As he returns, past a gawking Penny, and disappears into the back rooms, I say to my companions, "We have one religious zealot who likely hated Claire for her beliefs, and now we have a medical man who doesn't realize he is engaged in elder abuse. It seems to me he couldn't care less if these folks lived or died."

"Older people are ignored in our youth-oriented culture," Charlotte says, as we pass back down the extended halls. "Young folks enter a café or go to a concert, and their eyes skip over the silver-hairs as if they don't exist. They look for the young and the beautiful, the vigorous and the spry."

"Fear," Meredith adds. "They can't stand to see how they will someday look."

"What's their alternative?" I ask.

11

AFTER THE RAIN, a dense fog settles in around Bigelow Village as evening arrives. Mystery tales have conditioned me to think of fog as a cover for stealth, where bad guys hide and strike without warning from the darkness.

We eat in the cafeteria, which is good for me, because I see the various residents again, and it reminds me of their attitudes and beliefs. Charlotte is amazingly neutral about possible suspects in Claire's death. I am impatient and want to settle on one.

We walk back to Charlotte's apartment, and see a slip of paper taped to her door.

She unfolds it and reads:

YOU'RE NOT LISTENING.

"All right," I say. "This frightens me. I know you don't scare easily, but this idiot, whoever it is, is threatening you. I don't think you ought to be alone."

Meredith says, "Tell you what; I'll stay with you for the night, Charlotte. I have to go across the river to Trenton tomorrow for about three hours for a court hearing with a family I've been monitoring. But other than that, I can be with you."

My big sister waves her hand. "I don't need protection. But, I'm happy to have you spend the night with me–if you don't mind sleeping on the couch."

"My favorite spot," Meredith says.

"Why don't the two of us drive you to your motel, Greg. You need a good night's sleep too."

"The fog will make driving a challenge. Is there someplace in the complex where I can stay?"

"They have a rental apartment. I would have to see if it's available."

"Okay. It's not a matter of money," Greg says. "I want us all to be safe in this...hostile crucible."

"*Hostile crucible*—who would ever think a retirement village would earn that peculiar name?" Charlotte asks.

"Who would think," Meredith asks rhetorically, "a retirement village could harbor a killer?"

"If it's one of the residents we saw in the dining room, he or she would have had to slip away to post that little note. See anyone leave early?" I ask.

"People were coming and going," Charlotte says. "The note might have been left at any time in the hour we were there."

"Or, if anybody knew we were eating, an outsider could have delivered it," Meredith adds.

"The fog makes it unlikely that an outsider was observing us," Charlotte says. "Or, on the other hand, it could be the perfect camouflage for someone in a parked car, perhaps peering through windows and doors with binoculars."

"Yes," I reply, "and the moment he or she saw us leave for the dining hall, slip in and tape up the note."

"Lots of possibilities," Meredith says.

We amble over to the lobby, passing three or four folks moving about with walkers, and one in a wheelchair. They all know Charlotte and seem to brighten when she speaks to them. Brenda is the monitor at the desk, a middle-aged woman with a soft look and businesslike manner. She greets Charlotte agreeably.

"There's that sparkling lady," Brenda says. "What do you need?"

"Well, I'll get my mail from the slots back there, but also, my brother and I are wondering if your guest apartment is available for the night. He has a motel room, but wants to avoid traveling back there, at least for tonight."

"You're in luck. Trudy's grandson from Florida had reserved it, but his flight was cancelled today because of bad weather. It's seventy dollars, check or credit card."

The guest apartment is on the first floor, half way down a corridor that angles off to the left from the one that holds Charlotte's elevator.

She points it out and says, "You two go down and check it out. I'm going to get ready for bed."

I have a moment of trepidation: ought she to be going off alone, even for a few minutes? But since the halls are empty and no one seems to be stirring and Charlotte waves us away, I acquiesce.

The apartment has a queen-sized bed in one large room like Charlotte's—a small kitchen and a bath, neat and clean. A bowl is set out on the coffee table fronting the couch, containing an apple, an orange, and a banana. I wonder if the orange is from California. Where I live there was once a vast orange grove, perhaps fifty acres in all, and my property still contains three flourishing trees, navels, seedless, and delicious, which ripen each year near the end of November.

I am hoping that Meredith and I, being alone in a semi-intimate setting, might have a close moment, a moment that perhaps could jump-start our platonic relationship into something more. But, along with us, in the room, is the awareness that Charlotte might be targeted and is by herself—and I know Meredith is sensitive to that.

She says, "I'd love to spend a few minutes here just relaxing and talking with you, but I'm worried about Charlotte."

"Of course. Is there anything you need...I mean for the night...since you hadn't planned on staying here?"

"Well, I carry a spare toothbrush in my purse for just such occasions, and I'm sure Charlotte has soap and water and all that—and maybe even a pair of warm pajamas."

I feel like saying 'or not so warm ones,' as I realize that mention of sleep-wear stirs me, since I imagine Meredith undressing, so appealing in her nakedness, slipping into a loose nightgown, lying on Charlotte's sofa, soft, warm. Not that I haven't imagined her in such ways before.

Meredith turns to go, but spins about, and approaches me. Two feet away, she stops, looks deeply into my eyes, and says, "Greg, I want you to know how much I appreciate all that you and your sister are doing. You are dear people. I just love you both."

She leans forward and hugs me, hard, pulls slightly away, and kisses me, lightly, on the mouth. Then she smiles sweetly and says, "I'll get back to Charlotte. See you tomorrow."

Now, what do I do with that?

—

In the morning, close to 8:30, I walk over to the elevator, push the 'up' button and step out, across from Charlotte's room. All seems quiet and normal and I am hoping it is the same inside. I knock and she opens the door, scurrying at once back to her desk and computer.

"Come on in. There's coffee in the pot and some sweet rolls on the counter. Meredith was up and out of here by about eight." She seems absorbed at her keyboard.

"What's so intriguing?" I ask.

"Been investigating a few things. Did you know that researchers at Johns Hopkins have found that in the last decade, the mortality rate for older women has increased two-hundred-thirty percent from poisoning?"

"How would I know that?"

Ignoring me, she says, "A spokesman noted that the spike is traced to a dramatic rise in the use of powerful painkillers."

This catches my attention. "Aha! Another potential culprit in Claire's death."

"Have to be open to anything," she says.

Good, strong coffee. I sip and am quiet for a moment, as Charlotte says, "Another thing that might interest you: I checked the weather reports for yesterday and last night—interested in why Trudy's grandson could not get here."

"The desk clerk said it was weather."

"Yes, but she also said the young man was coming from Florida. There was no inclement weather in Florida all day and evening yesterday—except for a light rainstorm in St. Petersburg. And if it was supposed to be our local weather that grounded his flight, that also is hard to believe. Though we had some local fog, New York and Philadelphia, our two closest major airports, had virtually clear weather from three in the afternoon on."

"What are you getting at?"

"As the fisherman says, something smells fishy. Not with Brenda—she's only the messenger—but with Trudy's grandson wanting the apartment and then canceling."

"Trudy is the ninety-year-old with a cane?"

"That's right, and a cantankerous sort."

"So, what do you think is fishy?"

"Pure conjecture at this point, but it is possible that the man wanted to leave a record of having been unable to get here—when, in fact, he may have been here all along."

"Holy crap! Another possible scenario—but detectives could easily check out the passenger lists and find out if he was listed on one of them."

"The impression he may have wanted to give was for the Village, and he may have thought it would not get to any detectives…"

"Okay, but why? What would Trudy's grandson have to be stealthy about?"

"Don't know, but if I take a wild guess, it might be to quietly and secretly help Trudy with some caper she's involved in."

"Trudy, a ninety-year-old who walks with a wooden cane? You think she could be a suspect in all this?"

"Brother, until the perp is found, we're all suspects. Really, now, Trudy could hardly have executed some nefarious deed all by herself, though she could have thought one up and enlisted her grandson to carry it out, uh…persuaded him that she was somehow an injured party who needed redress. Sort of far-fetched, but not impossible."

"If that were the case, he would have to have been here for a couple of weeks, at least."

"Not out of the question," Charlotte says softly.

She focuses again on her computer, and, in a moment adds, "I also have learned that strokes are affecting more and more elderly folks without proper diagnoses—they are often mild or moderate, and go undetected and untreated, and then a stronger one occurs, like the straw that…well, you know."

"The autopsy will certainly reveal if Claire had a stroke."

"Yes, and it will also discover what, if any, of the several overdoses we've been learning about could be the culprit. I think the exhuming of the body might take place tomorrow. I'll check with Dr. Doolittle."

"I'm not letting you out of my sight today, just in case."

She touches my arm. "You're such a doting brother. Tell you what; let's go over to the workout room. This time of day, some twenty or more residents are involved in guided exercises. I'm pretty sure Trudy goes every day—and Freda as well."

It is a five-minute walk to the general elevator near the lobby desk, and we take it down to the basement level which houses a TV room, a bar (which seems unused), and at the far side a door marked GYM.

"This level is for recreation," Charlotte says. "On occasion, there is a birthday party or some other celebration, and they open the bar for wine and beer. No hard stuff."

Indeed, I see about two dozen folks, almost all women, some sitting on mats, others in wheelchairs, following the lead of a handsome, youthful, and sickeningly fit-looking coach. His voice is clear and strong, yet soothing.

Charlotte adds on, "Tomorrow at noon we are having a memorial for Claire in this area. We postponed it for a while, but the administration here doesn't like to drag things out. They say the residents need closure."

"A memorial? Who will speak, Char? You, I presume."

"I'll say a few words. The management will have an appropriate eulogy to present, and any of her friends, either in the Village or out, will be encouraged to speak."

"So, outsiders will be invited?"

"The people from New Hope who knew her will be coming, and perhaps our pharmacist, Oscar. I'm not sure about any of the MDs—they realize that folks here pass every couple of weeks, and they can't attend all the services."

"Morbid," I say.

"Not really. No one lives forever. The only thing about elder-care facilities is that all the residents are in the last quarter of their lives. Death is only a whisper away."

Internally I wince, since I am profoundly aware that Charlotte includes herself in that observation.

The coach, with his arms high over his head, says, "Five-minute break. No food. Water is okay. Don't go far. We start again at 9:10 on the dot."

He seems to recognize Charlotte and walks up to us.

"Hey, what a blast! All these beautiful people. Love to see 'em moving around. It'll help 'em to live longer. How come you're not out here?"

"I exercise in my room," Charlotte says, smiling at him, "and I walk a lot."

"Gotta fill those lungs. Gotta get that heart a-pumping. We're not sedentary creatures. If you don't use it, you lose it."

"I agree. Even our partially disabled folks can stir the blood with a workout."

"You got it. The body is a temple. Got to treat it with respect."

I am aware that this fellow—and as of this moment, I don't know his name—speaks in aphorisms. He is one well-conditioned cliché.

"This is my brother, Greg. This is Tommy Cox, our physical education coach."

We shake hands, his firm and meaty. He squeezes hard, almost to the point of pain, with a grin that says he knows what he's doing.

"Sorry about the old, blind gal who kicked off. She never wanted to do the routine. I told her once, *if you rest, you rust*, but she only laughed at me. Well, got to get back to my flock," he says. "Life is an adventure. Lots of these folks are on safari, unknown territory: exercise, for God's sake! Who'd believe it?"

When he leaves, Charlotte leans toward me. "He's goofy," she says. "Likes to pontificate. Not sure he quite appreciated Claire's situation. But, look there." She points to the opposite side of the large room, to a triangle of soft chairs around a low table. Seated in one of the chairs is a youngish man with blonde hair that splashes over his right eye. He wears a bright yellow and black sweater, jeans, and tennis shoes. He is tan, tall, and well built.

"I have a hunch," Charlotte says, "that we are looking at Trudy's grandson. We ought to go over and meet him."

The fellow rises dutifully as we approach, nods, and says, "I'm Sam Capizi, Trudy Langella's grandson."

"Charlotte and Greg Smart. I'm a resident, and my brother is a visitor."

He looks at us oddly, as if not sure why we are speaking with him. I defer to my sister, since she seems to know what she's doing and what to say.

"You're a visitor, too," Charlotte says. "When did you get in?"

"Get in?"

"To town. You're from down south somewhere—I can tell from your tan. Up here, by November, we lose ours; well, except for my brother here, who is from California."

Sam nods again, seemingly his standard act before speaking, and says, "I have business in New York, but decided to visit Grandma for a day or two."

"Oh," Charlotte says, "what kind of business?"

I am aware that he did not answer her first question.

"I'm in entertainment."

I am also aware of his parsimonious style. Taciturn, a man of few words.

"Movies, music, television, stage?" I put in.

"All of those. Promotion."

"Well, Sam Capizi, it was certainly a pleasure meeting you. Trudy is fortunate to have such a doting grandson," Charlotte says, and nudges me as if clinching that we are through and need to move on.

We stroll back across the room, circling the gaggle of exercisers, which has slightly diminished in number from before the break. Tommy Cox has an upbeat tape playing selections from *Music Man*: "Seventy-six-Trombones…"

He winks at us as we leave the room.

Out in the corridor, Charlotte turns to me. "Wild goose chase. That young fellow didn't do it."

"Do it? You mean Sam? He didn't kill Claire?"

"Right."

"How do you know that?"

"Timidity. Did you see his eyes? On the edge of fear; on the brink of panic. The perpetrator of this crime—pardon my French—needed balls. I could be wrong, but Sammy-boy, in there, is a mouse. I'll bet he only asserts himself if there's a monetary payoff, and I don't believe his assertion about being a promoter. My guess is he's a gofer. He may work in entertainment for an agency that does PR, but, with his attitude and personality, I'll lay odds he's the errand boy."

"You're not a gambler."

"Okay, so let's just say, my hunch is…what I said."

"He did seem rather terse."

"That's his style. Check his manner and you will see; he is uncomfortable in social settings. A behind-the-scenes worker bee, probably sent to New York as a messenger."

"How come I don't pick up any of that stuff?"

"When I get the chance, I'll consult with Trudy about him," Charlotte says. "Always like to double-check my perceptions. Meanwhile, we have only one day before the autopsy report and the memorial, so what do you say to living-it-up a bit? I propose that, as soon as Meredith returns, we head over to Princeton—it's just a forty-minute drive."

"I'd like that," I say. "Something elegant about Princeton."

My shrewd sister. Cross off one suspect.

12

THE FEW TIMES I have been to Princeton I have been charmed by the busy, yet unpretentious town, close enough to the prestigious university for faculty and students to walk over for coffee or lunch or an elegant dinner.

"How did it work out with the family you saw?" Charlotte asks.

Meredith, who volunteered to drive, finds a parking spot half a block off the main street, and we begin meandering about, gazing in windows. "As well as can be expected," she answers. "It's a case of almost certain child abuse, with two kids, nine and seven, the victims, and a frustrated stay-at-home mom, the beleaguered perpetrator. The father is gone a lot, a philanderer, and in a practical sense, the mom is trying to rear the children alone. The Department of Children's Services was called in, and I got the case. They gave contradictory addresses, so we had to meet on the New Jersey side."

"Kids at risk," I say. "I see it all the time in California. Overwhelmed families lashing out at the most vulnerable members."

"Terrible comment on our culture, isn't it," Charlotte notes in a cheerless voice, "that the very young and the very old are the most targeted victims."

"The least able to defend themselves," Meredith says.

We wander along the bustling streets, lined with novelty shops and cafes and funky coffee houses with indoor and outdoor seating. Despite the cool November weather, the outdoor seating areas are crowded with college students and others.

At one intersection, Charlotte says, "Ah, the beginning of the university just one block away. Let's hike up there. I want to visit the Princeton library."

Hmm. So, my mysterious sister had a private agenda for wanting to drive here. I might have known we didn't come here just for pleasure, and I wonder what critical information she's trying to track down now.

As we cross the street, we are surprised by a croaky voice that declares loudly, "Ho there, Charlotte!"

We turn and see Freda, the woman whom Charlotte says is an iconoclast, hustling toward us.

"Freda," Charlotte says, a trace of ginger in her voice, followed by a cajoling, "you followed us here."

"Didn't know you were coming," Freda says, sounding resentful.

I am impressed with her agility, movements crisp and rather energetic for a septuagenarian. Her motives are what my sister seems to impugn, and I wonder what comes next.

Breathless but undaunted, Freda cajoles back, "Four of us are here from Bigelow. We were invited to attend a chamber music event on the campus, but I decided to leave the others for a few minutes because…well, because those crotchety old battleaxes are boring."

"Chamber music?" Charlotte asks.

"Haydn and Mozart, two violins, a cello, and a viola. Free to folks over sixty-five. Starts in half an hour." She smiles, sort of ignores Meredith and me, and says to Charlotte, "You qualify."

"How nice, but we're here for other reasons," Charlotte says. Freda is the one resident of Bigelow Village my sister seems impatient with, though Trudy—as I have already seen—is also not one of her favorites.

"Suit yourself," Freda says. "By the way, old Trudy's grandson is a good-looking kid, don't you think?"

Since I hadn't seen Freda in the exercise room, I wonder why she presumes we have seen Sam Capizi.

Charlotte seems nonplussed and replies, "A tan Adonis from the deep South."

We walk away from Freda, our destinations in different parts of the campus, and Charlotte, always attentive to her companions, says, "A busybody, she is. You can see, she would have to have been spying on us to know we went into the exercise room."

"You sure have some odd birds living at Bigelow," I say.

"Yes, and Freda's constant vigil lends weight to her complicity in this whole affair, though I am not about to clinch that; it is still only one other possibility."

The Princeton library, located at One Washington Road, is an impressive edifice, and a haven for student-scholars and faculty, though the internet has, in recent years, become a competitor for uncovering research data. In the academic field, Princeton is one of the premiere research universities in the world. I feel a sense of reverence moving about on the campus. I imagine I would feel the same at Harvard or Yale, or perhaps Stanford on the West Coast.

Charlotte says, "You don't have to come in. I should only be about twenty minutes. If you like, take a stroll around; the grounds are wonderful."

Meredith and I agree, and drift over to the side of the library, where a grove of fir trees stand tall and green like perennial sentinels guarding their territory. The day is breezy, cold, and dry. We sit on the lawn, partly sheltered by a concrete parapet bolstering the massive building.

"I can't wait to hear what new angle Charlotte is examining. She is so damned creative about all this, you'd think she's been doing it all her life," I say. "But I know she hasn't."

"I wonder about this Freda woman. She is younger than her age, and has a lot of resentment. Claire hardly mentioned her, except to complain about how contrary she was."

"Well, I appreciate my sister's caution about conclusions. No matter what new evidence comes out—which sends me into a tizzy—she always seems tentative, which is a good thing. Of course, Freda *could* be a suspect, but then again we don't know for sure."

We are quiet for a time—I love the silence with Meredith, so connected in this moment, no contaminating noise or hyperbole, which most people insert when there is silence. At last, leaning on one elbow and looking me straight in the eye, she whispers, "You've never told me about your...uh, personal life in California. Relationships and such."

This is like a breakthrough! Of course, I've never told Meredith, because I have a fixation on her. And anyway, I haven't been in a relationship for several years—except the imaginary one in my mind, with her.

"Hmm. I'm a busy professional person with lots of male friends and colleagues. My...uh, personal life is, well, it's sort of moribund right now." I stop, and hurry to add, "By personal..." and here I take what for me is a huge risk, and add, "... do you mean romantic?"

She laughs. "That seems like a hard word for you. All right, romantic; no romantic entanglements?"

Love this topic. Chancy for me, but it is a leap in the right direction. I say, hopefully not in a pathetic way, "I've lost a couple of romances in the past. Made me kind of wary. Once bitten...you know."

"Aha, you look at your romances ending as negatives, as losses. It's true that vampires can bite, but I don't believe in them, so your amours must have had sharp teeth."

"I've yet been the one to end a relationship. I get entrenched and familiar, and hate the vacuum when things change."

She is thoughtful, and says, "When Theodore drowned, it was the worst vacuum I've ever known. I'm like you; it's hard to walk away from someone I've been close to, even if circumstances dictate it. It's taken a while, but I'm slowly learning to expel grief, to look forward."

As if speaking for her, I say, "So it's time to look around and see what else is out there."

For an instant she looks startled, then sits up straight and whispers, "Yes, that's it. There is a whole, interesting world out there, new people...even new romance, if I can be open to it."

"Can you?"

"I don't know," she retreats.

Students, most looking like high-schoolers, drift by us, chattering and restless, as the young tend to be. This is a college, but, perhaps because I am well into my middle age, and despite the influx of older folks returning to school, college students seem more like teen-agers to me, youthful, unsophisticated, antsy, and, from the language I pick up, totally irreverent.

I wait, and at last say, "I'm betting on you. You are an exquisite person. It would be impossible that someone wouldn't be out there eager to team up with a lovely woman."

Her smile tells me she is flattered, but what she says—her standard deflection—is, "Well, Greg, I think of you as my best friend. So, it makes sense you'd see me that way."

A bell begins to toll, the university carillon broadcasting that it is on the hour, though I see no reaction from any passersby. Don't they have to be in class when the big hand is straight up? I can't remember ever being late for a class. Too compulsive.

I'm about to say, "Is that all I am? Is a friend what I'm ordained to be?" but I hear Charlotte's voice from around the corner of the building.

"Yoo-hoo! Come out, come out, wherever you are."

Meredith calls back. "Over here. We're coming."

13

I AM EAGER to learn what new information Charlotte was seeking, but, typical of her, she moves on to the next focus, whatever her quick thoughts conjure up as the emerging need. Neither Meredith nor I ask for specifics, but Meredith does say, "I hope you found what you were looking for."

"Great library," Charlotte says. "We must push both Doolittle and Hartunian, the doctor for the autopsy report and the detective for the analysis of the pill bottles. Once we know what we're dealing with, we may come closer to fingering a possible suspect."

When we arrive at Bigelow, Charlotte tells us to stay put as she heads for the clinic, so Meredith and I are alone again, this time in my sister's apartment. I'm a bit concerned about Char going off alone, but it is the middle of the day and people are about—possible observers, a sure antidote for violence, since perps relish solitude and shadows.

But, before she leaves, Charlotte asks us a rather off-the-wall question. "Either of you ever take St. John's wort?"

I shake my head, as does Meredith, who replies, "Supposed to be a natural sort of Prozac, isn't it?"

"Might be," Charlotte says, in her usual mysterious manner, as she goes on her way.

"What was that all about?" I ask.

"I'll lay odds it was the subject of her library venture."

"I have folks in California who swear by St. John's wort—that it helps with their depression. But I know doctors who disagree. I've read in the professional journals about numerous side effects, some of them serious."

"I never heard Claire talk about taking it. Wonder why it's so interesting to Charlotte."

"We'll find out. Sooner if not later."

We don't know how long Charlotte will be gone, and I rev up my courage and say to Meredith, "You think of me like an older brother, don't you?"

"Older brother? Well, I never had a brother, but it might fit. I think of you as someone very close to me, a dear person, a wise friend."

"Yeah," I say. "I'm seventeen or eighteen years older than you. I suppose that gives me wisdom."

She looks at me oddly and says, "Age doesn't give wisdom. Experience helps, and insight is critical. Both you and your sister show keen insight into the world and people."

Me and my sister; alas, Meredith invariably retreats from the exclusive you-me topic.

"I'm good at my job, and that took training and involves heightened ability to see into people's pain. I guess you can call that insight. But I'll tell you something," and I feel pitiful saying this to her, "all the insight in the world doesn't substitute for a deep, loving relationship."

There. I laid it out. Wonder how she'll deflect that pronouncement and make it seem neutral.

After a quiet moment, Meredith begins to pace, turns suddenly, and says, "Greg, I am so sorry that your life is…well, unfulfilled. You always tell me how…exquisite you think I am, how desirable as a person—as a woman. Well, you surely are aware that you're the mirror of that on the male side. Someone would be a fool not to want you in her life."

"Someone?"

She flushes. I catch a reticence, an embarrassment. "Look, I'm not dense. It seems apparent that you are drawn towards me. It's my problem, not yours. I'm recovering from loss and am terrified to leap in—with any man. Maybe…well, I'm hoping that will begin to change. I want it to. But, right now, I need to put up the stop sign."

"Hey, I obey the traffic laws. Stop signs mean stop. I'm not pushing. But you're right-on about one thing: I am drawn towards you, and what I absolutely don't want is to put any kind of pressure on you, or do anything that would strain our connection."

"We have a lovely connection. I feel safe around you—and appreciated."

"I wish," I said, "that we didn't live three-thousand miles apart. Romance or not, we could go to the theatre together, concerts at the Disney Music Hall, opera at the Dorothy Chandler Pavilion. Hell, if you like sports, we could go to Dodgers games, or college football—UCLA or USC. The LA area is an entertainment mecca—and that's besides the mountains and beaches and desert."

She gives me a lovely smile and says softly, "Greg, I would love to be able to do those wonderful things with you. For now, you have your work there, and I have mine here."

I realize how prosaic our conversation is, how...well, stodgy is the word that comes to mind We are *discussing, conversing, chatting*. No passion in our words, an avoidance of emotion. Ah, nothing I can do about it. There is a bubble around her, and a hint of desperation in me. I want to take her sweet face in my hands and stare into her eyes and press my mouth onto hers. But, damn it, I'm aware that it ain't going to happen today!

Ought I to say, "It kills me that I'll be leaving in a few days and won't see you for months?" Ought I to say that? What's the use? When it's one way, love is a wild bull in a China shop, a torment, a well of loneliness—what one wag once called a dead-end street, a cul-de-sac.

I wonder what my clever sister would say if I unloaded all this on her?

As if thoughts of her cause it to happen, Charlotte walks in the door, a sly smile skewing her well-worn and still-handsome face.

"Got some more news," she says.

We sit in our same triangle and Charlotte lays her head back on the pillow of the sofa, eyes wide open, more in a posture of contemplation than fatigue. In fact, I can't recall Charlotte showing fatigue—amazing for a woman her age.

Slowly she begins to speak, as if by doing so, she is clarifying for herself.

"None of us saw Claire for at least two days prior to her death. Any symptoms she might have displayed from drugs or medicines could have developed in those couple of days, without detection. I, for one, saw no evidence of shakiness or distress the last time I was in her company." She pauses, lowers her head, and says, "Meredith, I presume you saw no changes in her as well?"

"Right. It was a week before she died that I last visited, and the only thing she said to me was that she had a migraine, and felt discouraged about something. When I asked what it was, her answer was a dismissive, 'Oh, nothing for you to worry about; a minor disagreement with another person.' I forgot about it almost at once, because she seemed not too concerned, and otherwise just the same as always."

"Yes," Charlotte says. "But, as with all little dropped hints, we need to keep that minor disagreement statement in the backs of our minds, since I'm sure it will surface again."

"I can certainly imagine a disagreement with Freda, or even Trudy," I say.

"Or a dozen other folks who get testy when they are frustrated," Charlotte says. "Like someone–*anyone*–getting served ahead of them in the dining hall, or Claire getting mail from Brenda at the desk first, because of her blindness. Resentment often obscures disabilities."

"But, what are you angling for?" I ask. "I mean about Claire seeming different shortly before her death?"

"Some of the leads we've been following, with medications wrongly managed, would have shown symptoms, a build-up of what the labels cite as side-effects. None of us noticed any symptoms. That doesn't eliminate toxic combinations as a cause, but it does narrow the list."

"You asked us about St. John's wort," Meredith says. Do you think Claire was taking that as a supplement?"

"Let me back up a bit and explain it this way. Serotonin is a key neurotransmitter that regulates appetite, mood, pain, and sleep. Serotonin deficiency is a leading cause of depression and is often treated with antidepressants like Zoloft or Prozac."

"So," I interrupt, "how does that relate to St. John's wort?"

"Too much serotonin can lead to serotonin syndrome, which is potentially life threatening and can cause agitation, vomiting, and sometimes disorientation. Serotonin syndrome occurs when antidepressants are combined with other supplements–for example, triptans, which are used to treat migraines, or St. John's wort. In the Princeton library, I found a solid article warning against combining an antidepressant with St. John's wort"

"How is that dangerous?" Meredith asks.

"Both help raise serotonin levels in the brain, and serotonin syndrome could lead to seizures or strokes."

"And possibly without a long lead-time of symptoms?" I ask.

"That's right. I asked Doolittle about that, and he said there is a threshold, and once it is reached, the symptoms would flare. Until it's reached, the syndrome flies below the radar."

"Since fibromyalgia patients know all about serotonin-enhancing drugs, the woman at the Vision-Aid place, Helen Cumberland, and Freda here at Bigelow, would have the sophistication to know about lethal combinations," Meredith says.

"Well yes, but keep in mind," Charlotte replies, "that I do not have fibromyalgia, and it took me only a few minutes of research in the library to learn about all this."

"So," I say, resignedly, "we're no closer to unmasking a culprit than we were before."

"Perhaps not," Charlotte says, "but I have more to tell you. Before turning over the pill bottles to Detective Hartunian, I carefully raised the braille paste-on labels and peeked at the prescription labels underneath. I had found, in Claire's room, a translation chart listing the alphabet equivalents to braille figures."

"Wearing those rubber gloves, I'll bet," I say.

"You got it. And sure enough, a couple of the labels underneath were not the same as the braille labels covering them. In fact, they had been reversed. The braille label on one read *Triptan, for migraines*, and underneath, it read *St. John's wort*. On the bottle that noted *St. John's wort, triptan* was listed on the original label. Besides all that, Claire was taking selenium and the steroids Overstreet had been giving her. All in all, a toxic package of supplements."

"Then we have to uncover who actually switched the labels," I say. "The tall lady at Vision Aid may have resented Claire's nonreligious stance, but would that be enough to trigger lethal mischief?"

"Not likely," Charlotte says. "But let us keep an open mind about it."

"It does seem crucial to learn the actual cause of death," Meredith says. "You say the autopsy results may be ready soon?"

"Dr. Doolittle says the body has been exhumed and the autopsy is underway. He hopes to know by tomorrow."

"The same day as the memorial service," I add.

"Just like in the movies," Charlotte declares in a mock pompous tone, "most of the suspects will be present."

"Except, you said, for the medical doctors, one of whom could be the perpetrator," Meredith notes.

"And the Cumberland woman. No reason for her to attend," Charlotte adds.

"But, if she does…?" I let the notion hang in the air.

"Juicy development," Charlotte says.

14

"CRAP, CRAP, crap!" Trudy utters loudly, sitting at the table across from ours. "I hope you don't mind," she peers over at us through rheumy eyes, and says, "that I swear. My dear husband never let me swear, but Sammy here, my understanding grandson, doesn't try to stop me."

Sammy is seated with her, both seeming to be drinking coffee, their lunch plates empty of food, yet, with the poor service, left languishing on their table.

"What are you swearing about, Trudy?" Charlotte asks.

For a moment, she seems to have forgotten, then, in a burst of venom, shouts, "It's not fair! I don't have any...future."

It would be funny, I think, if it were not so sad. Elderly folks live with a very present-oriented approach to life. Trudy, being ninety, considers the final few years of a person's existence as unjust, a betrayal of the essence of the journey, which ought to promise, as Tennyson wrote, "...a work of noble note (that) may yet be done."

"Good food, an attractive grandson, friends, warm surroundings—these are your present and your future," Charlotte says.

"Yes," Trudy replies, softly, her pronouncement lost to memory, her ire gone, the look in her eyes saying that she is not sure what my sister is talking about. Could a person with memory issues be a plotter in a murder?

Across the room, Freda is sitting by herself at a table, intent on a bowl of what could be the cold strawberry soup Charlotte once praised–at least it looks reddish from a distance.

It is past one o'clock, and the memorial for Claire is set for two, downstairs, in the exercise room, which has been reconfigured with some sixty chairs set in rows like a school auditorium. Before that, in about ten minutes, Charlotte is to meet with Dr. Doolittle in the medical offices, to review the autopsy report. Char invites the two of us to join her, but Meredith and I decide against it, opting instead to take a walk and hear the results later.

When we are alone, wandering toward the front counter area where Brenda stands, Meredith says to me, "Did you see Freda, sitting all alone? She's an odd duck all right. I wouldn't put anything past her."

Charlotte's admonition about keeping an open mind resounds in me. "Yes," I reply, "but, there would have to be a clear motive. She may be a maverick among these elderly folks, yet I don't know why she would want to harm Claire. Unless…" I hesitate before finishing, "…she has some sort of clandestine history with her that we know nothing about."

Meredith nods. "She's creepy, shows up at odd places, seems to be in on everything, and she's vigorous enough to carry out a lot of mischief."

As we pass the counter, Brenda looks up, sees us, and says, "Be going downstairs in a bit. Good thing to honor Claire."

Brenda has a strong Boston accent, an 'r' pronounced like 'ah'–for some reason I always relate New England accents to being well educated, which is a foolish generalization. She is a slim woman, except for her upper arms, which sag and are flabby. Often, her voice is laced with impatience.

"Had a tough go of it," Brenda continues, "with her extreme views and all."

I step over and place my hands on the counter. "Tell me, Brenda, what do you mean by *her extreme views and all?*"

"Oh, like never going to services and that. These older folks are set in their ways. Hard to tolerate the unusual or the unknown."

"Any idea which old folks might have resented her?"

"I steer clear of the resident tangles. Wouldn't do for me to take sides or even agree with anyone's arguments. I stay neutral."

She clasps her hands behind her head–I see the limpness of her upper arms–and the posture seems, somehow, to contradict the words.

"Yes," I say, "but, do you know who might have been at odds with Claire?"

"Well…can't be sure, but old Trudy is a devoted religious person and, when she could remember, would complain about Claire. And, let's see, do you know Freda? She likes to take the opposite side of anything. That's just her style."

"Ah. Anyone else?"

"Maybe. Not sure you know Elmore, who suffers from dementia. Well, his wife is orthodox Jewish and she has trouble with anyone who is different. I've heard her arguing with some of the Catholic residents. Silly, if you ask me."

"I agree," Meredith says. "Arguing about religion is indeed silly."

"Thanks," I nod to Brenda. "See you downstairs."

We move toward the small library room where we once saw Freda sitting, and I say to Meredith, "Did you see all the little posters on the wall behind Brenda? She is like a living ad for Hallmark cards; sayings and gushy advice-giving, and even words that could have come from a Chinese fortune cookie: 'You are admired for your good work,' and 'People are drawn towards your warm personality.' Oddly, though, I don't see Brenda's personality as being warm, and she is the farthest thing from a holiday greeting."

"I agree. My guess is she knows a lot more than she lets on. After all, she dispenses all the mail and packages that arrive."

"We'll have to ask Charlotte about her. It seems pretty remote that she would be a suspect when it comes to Claire's death, but she sure-as-hell could know who might be."

There, in the library, in the same chair, again reading what appears to be the *New York Times*, is Freda. She smiles at us enigmatically and briefly before disappearing behind a wall of newsprint.

—

We are about to enter the elevator down to the bottom level when Charlotte catches up with us. She is a bit out of breath, seeming to have hurried back from her visit with Dr. Doolittle.

"Beautiful day," she says between deep inhales. "Love it in November when we have sunlight and clear skies and the dappled seasonal colors."

When the elevator door closes, she whispers: "Stroke. The autopsy showed a severe rupture in the brain. The doctor referred to it as a cerebrovascular incident." She probably died instantly. Thank goodness for that."

The doors open and Charlotte finishes with, "There's more, but I'll have to tell you later."

—

Soft music hovers in the room, which is filling with walkers, wheelchairs, and slowly moving residents–along with the slightly younger, brisk and determined folks, striding smartly as if to prove a point. I see Wally Burt in the second row; seated alongside him is Delbert, the fellow who owns the Go Fur It shop, and next to him a wispy woman, looking rather unkempt, though with a certain attractiveness, most likely Delbert's wife.

In the third row, close to the exit is Oscar Ott, the pharmacist, seated where he will be able to make an early exit.

Charlotte is motioned to a chair along the wall, reserved for the speakers; she points to the two of us, and the residential director, a husky woman with closely cropped, dyed black hair, dressed in a vest and long, tan trousers, bustling about with an air of authority, nods her assent.

The room fills, and the director taps on the microphone, hears the electronic clicks, and says, "Welcome, lovely people. As you know, we are gathered here to honor one of our dear, long-term residents, Claire Hazelton, who left us suddenly a week or so ago."

I wonder if the eulogies–at least some of them–will be religious in tone, or if the speakers, knowing Claire's disposition, will refrain from other-worldly references and heaven-hell pros and cons. My question is answered at once.

"Dear Claire has joined her maker," the director, Doreen by name, says to the assembly. "Considering her afflictions and disabilities, we can appreciate that she is now in a far better place. And though we mourn her passing, as we do all our dear companions here at Bigelow Village, we are comforted by the knowledge that Claire Hazelton, as will one day happen to every one of us, has now gone home for her eternal rest."

Tilt! I think those are the wrong things to be saying to a room full of octogenarians. Morose. Depressing. I glance at Meredith, who is trying to look impassive, but I catch a narrowing of her eyes and the beginning of a scowl around her mouth.

Charlotte nudges me with her knee, a slight smile turning her lips upward at the corners.

"As we like to do," Doreen continues, "the Board has bequeathed a donation to a charity of Claire's choice, and, since her death was sudden, we shall consult with her lovely granddaughter," she nods her head toward Meredith and smiles sweetly, "about the dispensing of the gift."

She pauses, I presume to let the impact of the Village's generosity sink in.

"And now, we open our memorial service to those who wish to speak about Claire Hazelton and her long and fruitful life. The first speaker will be our own Charlotte Smart."

My sister walks slowly to the microphone, smiles broadly at the attentive crowd–though I do see a couple who seem to be dozing–and begins.

"I would like to celebrate a life, not a death. Life is precious, and Claire's was full and rewarding in many ways. She was an achiever, and, as many of you know, a woman with intense passions. I consider myself fortunate to have been counted as one of her friends."

I gaze about the room to see if anyone shows an antipathy to Charlotte's words, any scowling or headshaking. I doubt one would be foolish enough to display open dissent, especially one who might be the architect of her demise. Freda seems preoccupied with her hand, maybe a hangnail; Trudy's eyes are closed but she is sitting upright and appears to be tuning in; her grandson, Sam, is peering out the window; Oscar Ott is nodding slowly, as if in agreement; Elmore and his wife (I never did learn her name), the one Brenda said was orthodox Jewish, are staring hard at Charlotte, though Elmore's eyes are wider than normal, most likely struggling to comprehend; Wally and Delbert, his fellow entrepreneur from New Hope, look thoughtful and serious; Delbert's wife, oddly enough, is crying.

"Yes, her passing is a shock, because it was so unexpected. She was engaged in life up to the end of hers–and that is a message to us all. No one needs to preach to you about the meaning of life; all of us here at Bigelow are the veterans of the world, having lived long and experienced widely. One thing, however, I do want to share. At any moment, we are confronted with choices. Like a stone tossed in a river, once we have chosen we cannot lasso our choice and pull it back. Claire's amazing life was filled with elegant choices, though I am quite aware that there may be some here who might disagree."

Again, I look about, to see reactions. There is an intense silence in the room, Charlotte's words like a benevolent yet firm hand closed around the entire gathering, holding them in rapt attention. Doreen, the Village administrator, has made her hands into a prayer position and is nodding solemnly.

"She was an independent thinker, this Claire Hazelton, her beliefs all her own, and yet she was never an evangelist, never attempted to convert or convince anyone else. She was a true lover, and she loved whomsoever she chose to love, whether others approved or not. All of us do that, yet, in her case, because her choices fell outside society's mainstream, Claire was often indicted. And for what? ...*For the way she loved!*"

She says those last five words with piercing ardor, each word separated and stressed. For a moment she is silent, as if letting the meaning of her message sink in.

"If we live long enough, we will suffer painful losses," she resumes. "That is the bane of being human and having extravagant consciousness—which no other species can claim. Yet, we would have it no other way. We live, we celebrate, we love, we suffer, and we remember. The positives must balance out the negatives; our days must not be dragged down with depression and grief, so I call on all of us here, myself included, to rejoice over Claire Hazelton's remarkable, beautiful, and exquisite life!"

As I gaze about the room, I see standing just inside the door, leaning against the wall, Detective Augie Hartunian, arms crossed, chin thrust upward, eyes darting back and forth, taking in the audience reaction. The Mounties to the rescue, I think.

15

THREE OTHERS speak about Claire, all strangers to me. They are pleasant and complimentary, and simply nice. Nothing negative is presented, and that is almost always the case at a memorial–though I remember that Marc Anthony did say, "I come to bury Caesar, not to praise him."

Hartunian approaches after the program has ended. Serious as a prowling bear, he says, "I understand you folks have been doing some private investigations. Remember, I cautioned you about that."

"What do you mean?" Charlotte asks.

"Considering what you passed on to me, I have been in touch with the doctors here, and they have told me you have been...well, meddling. Now, even though I'm upset, we must share information, or we are working at cross-purposes. I doubt that you know more than I do, but tell me what you know."

The Village administration has set out a buffet table at the far end of the hall, and the crowd is now gathering to partake of baby carrots, broccoli, cherry tomatoes, celery stalks, and a variety of cookies, along with plastic cartons of apple and cranberry juices. I am eager to stroll among the crowd to hear comments, but Hartunian has us captured for the moment.

"Officer Hartunian," Charlotte says, "we have only been asking questions. After all, Claire was dear to us, and we want to get to the bottom of all this."

"Yes ma'am, but if there is a killer among us, you are setting yourself up for a bumpy ride."

"Indeed, Detective," I say, "Charlotte has received another warning note. I do worry about her safety."

"Let me see the note," he asks.

"It's in my apartment," Charlotte says. "I don't take these little warnings too seriously. Someone did a terrible thing, and of course is worried that he, or she, will be discovered. I can't imagine I would be threatening to anybody. After all, I am a total amateur and have no expertise in tracking down criminals."

"If criminals thought logically, I would agree with you, but they don't. That's what makes them lawbreakers; they think outside the box. For the bad guys, survival is everything."

Charlotte smiles and says, "For all of us, really."

Hartunian's little lecture is interrupted by Elmore's wife, who walks up and says, "Charlotte, your words were splendid. I think it is very important for people to…live and let live."

"Thank you, Esther. I appreciate your comment. I hope your husband is doing okay."

"As well as can be expected. Ronald Reagan lived for ten years with Alzheimer's. It's a sad way to spend your later years, but, so far, he seems happy enough."

Esther sees her husband gabbing with a woman in a wheelchair, chuckling and looking pleased with something he must have said. "Must monitor Elmore," she says, turning away from us. "He does okay for a couple of minutes, then fear sets in and he forgets where he is."

"I'll tell you this," Charlotte says to Hartunian, "Dr. Doolittle passed on to me that the cause of death was an infarction in the brain. In other words, a blockage that led to a stroke."

"Yes, I managed to retrieve that information as well, but then why do we presume there was treachery?"

"Because there was," Charlotte says, pleased she knows more than the police. "The cerebrovascular event was caused by an excess of supplements in her system. That is the next challenge: to discover which additives were overdosed and who deliberately did it. And, if we get that far, to uncover the *why* behind it all."

Hartunian grins. "Little lady, you are one clever cookie. I might decide to hire you on my team. I've got a couple of hot-shot officers who could learn a thing or two from you."

Wally Burt wanders up, accompanied by his entrepreneur neighbor, Delbert, and his somber-looking wife.

"Ah, Charlotte," Wally says, "you are a jewel, a treasure. Your message is inspirational. Claire's essence was never better captured." He pauses briefly. "I believe you know Delbert Kraus and his wife, Evangeline. We all loved Claire deeply."

"Yes," Delbert adds. "We were not as familiar with her as Wally, but we did know what a special woman she was."

Evangeline's eyes dart about, restless, dark. She says nothing, but her mood is clearly one of agitation. Without being too obvious, I check on Charlotte, and see she is concentrating on Evangeline.

"I dare say," my sister throws out, "that Claire's passing has affected all of us deeply, even those who encountered her occasionally. That woman had a powerful presence."

I also watch Hartunian to see if he has any inclinations, one way or another, about any of the folks at the gathering. That's what cops are supposed to do: develop hypotheses and follow hunches. He seems intent on the snacks, and, in a moment, leaves us and begins to partake of them. Doubtless he regards our conversation as little more than the camaraderie of old folks. I don't think of him as dull, but he seems often to be on a tangential track.

Freda steps over to our little group, and says to Charlotte, "Where'd you find the gumshoe?"

"Who?" Charlotte says, feigning surprise.

"Doesn't hide his vocation very well. I can spot 'em every time."

Wally and Delbert show a moment of confusion: wrinkled brows, slight tilt of their heads, looks of curiosity sent Charlotte's way.

"Oh, it's a routine thing. This particular officer was assigned to oversee the passing. They often do that, you know, check into deaths to be sure they are purely natural."

"I was talking with him," I add. "Nice fellow. In fact, his uncle lives in California, and I had occasion to run into him."

"Well," Wally says, "I presume that Claire's death was natural, was it not? What else could it be?"

Meredith is silent, yet I see her studying the several faces in our little cluster, her own face stern and pensive. Even with her grim demeanor, I am struck by her loveliness. Well, yes, of course, because I am in love with her.

Someone has turned on a speaker system and the tones of an old song, "Always in My Heart," begin to fill the room.

"Really," Charlotte says. "What else could it be?"

"We must get back to our store," Delbert says. "A teenager is holding down the fort for us, and it might be over his head."

Softly, almost inaudibly, Evangeline says, "He is in over his head. Can hardly count out the change. Pleasant enough, but dense."

"Yes," Wally adds. "I too must return to business. As you so elegantly put it, Charlotte, life does go on, and we must continue to celebrate it."

Wally's one gray eye seems so much more pronounced under the glare of the overhead tube lighting. I wonder how well he drives, and if he drives at night. Suspicious me—I keep remembering what Charlotte says, that we must have an open mind, and that anyone can be a suspect.

After the three New Hope folks depart, I ask Charlotte, "What's with the wife, Evangeline? She seems gravely depressed."

"I don't know her well, only met her a couple of times, but my impression is the same as yours: depression. She and Delbert have been married about ten years, and I think he has had to deal with it a few times—with therapy, I mean."

"So," Meredith says, "looking about, with all these folks here, what do you think, Charlotte? Is there any light shining on who the culprit may be?"

"You sound as if you might have a thought or two," Charlotte replies.

"I do. I think that nasty Freda is in the lead." She points at the buffet where Freda has gone to sample the offerings, and is conversing with Hartunian. "She is crafty and tries to be accommodating, but there is something under the veneer, something a bit too facile about her."

"Yes, well, I agree with all you've said. It remains to be seen if Freda had enough animosity to turn her feelings into action. She certainly seems to pop up at the oddest places and with the most piercing comments."

"Is there someone else you think is more likely?" I ask.

"There are several more aspects of this situation that need to be unstrung, and I'm hoping Hartunian will be more focused than he has been today. Meanwhile, Trudy and her grandson are fading, in my opinion—not enough savvy, not enough guts. I don't for one-minute suspect Wally. He really did love Claire. His cross-the-street neighbor, Delbert, did not know Claire well enough to want to do her harm, and his wife's tears, I imagine, are for herself, since she is a troubled personality. Esther, the woman with the Alzheimer's husband, could be gaming us with her compliments about my little talk. She is, after all, committed to her orthodox religion, and knew that Claire was not the least bit religious."

"I thought you said that Claire did not broadcast her atheism. If so, then how would...?"

"True, but I have heard her say—without trying to tone down her voice—that she appreciated George Gershwin's *Porgy and Bess* lyrics that what's written in the Bible 'ain't necessarily so.' And Gershwin, as we all know, was Jewish, so our rather rigid friend, Esther, could have heard all that and resented both George and Claire as being heretical."

"Wow," Meredith says. "The intrigue is overwhelming. Your analysis puts a lot into perspective, but doesn't settle anything."

"No," Charlotte replies, with a distant look. "But, I'll tell you, I sort of wished that Dr. Lyle Overstreet had been in attendance. His general indifference about the elderly is a flashing neon sign, indicating more animosity toward Claire than any of us could know. I, for one, would have been fascinated to observe his reaction to all this."

She gets another unfathomable look in her eye, and adds, "And Helen Cumberland, the woman who translated the pill labels, may have known nothing about Claire's sexual preferences, but, from her parting comment that day in her office, I believe that she knew about Claire's spiritual beliefs. And Helen has been taking painkillers for fibromyalgia, has been here, and is aware of the layout of the Village."

"I recall something Maya Angelou once said, which I share with my students: 'There is a world of difference between truth and facts. Facts can obscure the truth.'"

"Excellent," Charlotte bubbles. "She also said that it is important that we '...recognize and celebrate our heroes and she-roes!'

Meredith laughs out loud.

I am surprised to see, standing just outside the door, peering in, Tommy, the muscular exercise instructor.

16

CHARLOTTE SENDS me on an errand, to buy some gin and tonic water, "Because," she says, "we need to mellow out." I think she wants to be alone with Meredith.

When I return to her apartment, she greets me with a wide grin, grabs my parcel, and scurries into the kitchen area. Meredith is seated on the sofa, head back, eyes closed, mouth in a beatific smile. I wonder what in hell went on.

As soon as we are all settled with gin and tonics, I say, "You said in there that you had more information for us from Dr. Doolittle."

"I do. Since Claire's death was caused by a severe stroke, I asked Doolittle what, of all the additives she seemed to be taking, could cause such a catastrophic event. He noted that, of course, stroke is a possible result of serotonin syndrome, which can occur when a new medication is added to ones already taken, such as St. John's wort. An excess of selenium in the system, as we have already discussed, can be lethal. The autopsy showed high amounts of both St. John's wort and selenium.

"While that doesn't clinch which one caused her death, it does zero in on at least a couple, and sort of diminishes steroids, which Dr. Overstreet kept prescribing—though it does not eliminate them completely, because steroids, cumulatively, can cause bodily trauma."

"But, since the labels were switched on the bottles, she certainly took the wrong amounts of whatever pills she was using. That pretty much commands us to pin down who switched the labels," I say.

Charlotte seems thoughtful, yet says glibly, "You got it. We know that Wally's prints are on the bottles, but since he was her friend, he could have innocently given her pills from the wrong bottles. If he had been doing that deliberately, he surely would have worn gloves or somehow erased his prints. Remember, Helen Cumberland wore gloves on the day we met her."

She stops, but, in a moment adds, "Since the labels were switched, it is also possible that Claire wrongly medicated herself. Terrible to think of that, but, in any case, it would still be murder."

"Hmm, Grandmother had a lot of people in her life that I knew nothing about," Meredith says. "Because of their own particular resentments, more than one could have wanted to do her harm."

"Yes," Charlotte says, "and you know what," she turns to face me, "while you were gone, Greg, I arranged with the Village administrators for a merchant's fair to take place this Friday. We have them two or three times a year, and we invite in local entrepreneurs to display their wares, so Village residents don't have to travel to make purchases. The fall fair is usually closer to Christmas or Chanukah, and we contact businesses in Newtown and Langhorne, the closest little hamlets to us. But, for this gathering, I would also like to invite the business people we know from New Hope. Wally Burt can transport his pies and other yummy baked goods, and Delbert Kraus can bring in his faux furs and stylish clothing."

"The idea being?" I ask.

"The idea being to gather together as many suspects as possible to see what we can cook up."

"So, the Village occupants will all be here—including any people we have suspicions about—and some of the outsiders as well," Meredith says. "I do recall Claire mentioning these gatherings, and she appreciated them because she had a hard time getting out into the community."

"I want Helen Cumberland and my pharmacist friend, Oscar Ott, to attend. I wager both will come, since the business folks give breaks in price when they set up here. And, besides all of them, I will also encourage the medical staff, Overstreet and Doolittle, to swing by and check out the bargains, along with Brenda, our desk and mail person—though I hardly think of her as a suspect in all this—and Tommy, our exercise guy."

"Man," I say, "we'll likely have every possible person here who could have done the deed. But, I still don't know how you plan to confront them, or at least have them interact. After all, the purpose is to try to expose who might have doctored the pill containers."

"I'm working on that. You know the adage that criminals like to return to the scene of the crime. I'll bet my new bottle of gin that somebody will tip his or her hand."

"What's difficult to know," Meredith says, "is how many of these folks might have visited Claire in her apartment, and… well…*helped* her with her meds."

"Despite her strong beliefs and preferences, Claire was a social person," Charlotte adds, as if thinking aloud. "My guess is that she had a lot more visitors than we could have imagined."

"Too bad there are no security cameras," I say. "We'd see a hell of a lot if that were the case."

"Invasion of privacy," Charlotte responds. "I would fight that if they even hinted at wanting to install them."

We are all silent, and I hear the whoosh of an incipient wind beginning to agitate the almost leafless tree limbs outside Charlotte's windows. I shiver, since it seems to be a cold gust, and I wonder if this Pennsylvania locale will see its first snow before I return to California.

"I shall also invite Augie Hartunian," Charlotte says, staring out the window.

I am scheduled to return home on Sunday and, beyond all sensibility, I presume that my sister, perhaps with Hartunian's assistance, will unmask the villain before I leave. Charlotte's brassy shrewdness has me mesmerized. In some inconceivable way, she seems to know exactly what needs to be done. Where in hell did she acquire that skill? I certainly don't have it. Many of her insights and proposals catch me totally by surprise.

After a few gin and tonics, and some casual conversation about the Lambertville Musical Theatre–an outdoor amphitheater on the Jersey side we used to frequent as youngsters and where saw Victor Herbert musicals, Nelson Eddy, and Jeanette McDonald–Meredith drives me back to my motel. She is about to depart, but first smiles her appealing smile, leans toward me in the car, and kisses my cheek.

"What?" I ask.

"Your sister is a wise lady," she says, with a tone of mystery.

"I know."

Meredith's lips spread in what now looks to be an inscrutable smile, as she says, "She tells me I would be well advised to step back, take a few deep breaths, and try to reassess my old wounds."

"Well, yes, but…"

"No buts about it," she interrupts. "I'm working on it."

I hesitate, and finally say, "When you've got it all figured out, Meredith, I hope you'll clue me in."

"You'll be the second person to know."

"And the first is?"

"Silly man, me!"

—

At 5:00 AM the phone in my motel room rings. I lift the receiver and Charlotte says, "There were just loud knocks on my door. I was afraid to open it so I waited. After a couple of minutes, I inched it open and saw another of those notes."

"Holy crap! Are you okay?"

"I'm fine, but the note read: Meddlers pay the price!"

17

I PHONE MEREDITH at 8:00 AM. She agrees to call into her office to request a personal leave day, pick me up, and hurry over to Bigelow Village. We both feel deep regret that we left Charlotte alone.

We arrive at nine and, a few minutes later, Augie Hartunian knocks on Charlotte's door. When we show him the newest note, he blurts out, "Mary, mother of Jesus! We've got a true psycho on our hands. This yo-yo could get real nasty."

"That's why you're here," I say, "to keep that from happening."

"It is a leap up in chutzpah," Charlotte says, "since he or she deliberately roused me from sleep to get my attention, and then had to quickly disappear before being seen. My guess is that he left the elevator door propped open so the escape could be quick."

"What's frustrating is that it could be a resident in the Village, or it could be an outsider," Meredith says.

"Did you happen to hear a car start up and drive away?" I ask.

"My apartment is on the opposite side from the parking area. I never hear the cars. At five in the morning, the person might well have left the motor running, hustled in, did the work, and disappeared in seconds." She stops, and adds, "*If* it was an outsider."

Hartunian has been silent, listening to our repartee, and finally, with a burst of insight, says, "The letters on this note are from a news-paper, carefully cut out. I'm pretty sure that a man wouldn't take the time to do such a thing. This creep has to be a woman."

My sister smiles and replies, "Desperate people will do a lot of things to camouflage their trail. A woman would want us to think it is a man; a man would want us to think it is a woman."

"Hmm, yes, I suppose you're right," Hartunian admits, in his reticent, noncombative way.

"Is there some way you can assign an officer to watch over Charlotte?" I ask.

"We have a small staff, but I could have my assistant, officer Antonia Clay–Toni for short–hang around the area a few hours a day, kind of keep her eyes open, see what's going on. I'll instruct her to wear street clothes instead of her uniform."

"Better than nothing," Meredith says.

"I'll bet Freda will smell her out anyway," I say.

The ring of Charlotte's phone startles us–she keeps it on high since her hearing, she tells me, is not as good as it used to be.

"Hello. Oh, Wally. Yes, it's this Friday at ten o'clock. It'll be in that same auditorium on the first floor. I know, but the folding chairs will all be put away." She listens. "Well, I'm not sure of the actual numbers, but I expect a pretty hefty turnout." Again, she listens. "We all look forward to seeing you–and bring a lot of those wonderful pastries."

Charlotte turns back to us. "So far, he's the only one who's called. That's not so unusual, since those from the other nearby towns have come to these fairs before and already know the routine."

"Clue me in, little lady," Hartunian says.

"I've arranged for a community merchant fair. Expect a few dozen local businesses to set up their wares. It's a good way to get a lot of folks here at one time and see if anything unusual goes on."

Hartunian nods and says with a pensive look, "Clever, clever, Ms. Smart, but maybe not smart. It could be dangerous. Think I'll plan to be here. Meanwhile, I'll have forensics check over this note for prints or other clues."

"Wonderful, Augie. The four of us make a remarkable team."

Looking pumped up, perhaps because of the slanted compliment, Hartunian heads toward the door, and leaves us with, "Watch your backs, all of you. We're going to get this sicko. I can promise you that."

When he is gone, Meredith says, "Promises, promises."

I look at Charlotte, wondering what her cunning mind is conjuring up as the next move. As always with my sister, I am not disappointed.

"Look," she says with eerie fervor, "it would be good if the two of you could do this: nose about, wander through the central lobby, check out the front desk, peruse the dining area, peer into the library, visit the exercise room—in short, as they say in the crime movies, case the whole joint. See if anyone acts cagey, belligerent, arrogant, or shows any other odd manner. If it is someone from Bigelow, I am convinced his or her hand will be tipped."

"And you?" I ask. "Where will you be?"

"Ah," she says in her wonderfully mysterious and impossible-to-read style, "I have a bit of important work to do. Claire's apartment beckons. We might have overlooked some absolutely critical evidence right in front of our noses. After all, she was a collector of all kinds of items from friends and fellow residents, and hardly ever threw things away."

"Freud," I say, "once believed that the nose was the key to our sexuality. He later changed his mind."

"It's a figure of speech, since, compared to most animals, we humans are woefully deficient in olfactory sensitivity. Though I will tell you this: as I've grown older, my nose has grown, and wouldn't it be salutary if the bigger it gets the more acute its capability?"

"Kind of odd," Meredith tosses out, "but all this talk about noses has made me hungry. Maybe we can catch some breakfast food in the dining area."

"Sure. If they ask, tell them you are my guests.

"You're full of appetizing tidbits," I say.

—

Two hours later I learn something critical, reported by Charlotte. But, first, I will say that Meredith and I felt like phony sleuths, trying hard to look innocent, cruising about the residence byways like a couple of tourists. We saw nothing startling, and the only perception we decided might be important to tell Charlotte was that we observed Freda, sitting at a table in the dining hall, with Esther Hahn and her husband, Elmore. Elmore, of course, was gazing about the room vacuously, but the two women had their heads together, as if sharing jokes—or secrets. Or, possibly, it was Freda pontificating, since she seemed to have some disdain for Elmore, and, more than likely, for Esther as well.

When I describe to Charlotte what we observed, she nods dutifully, at which point I catch that she wanted us off somewhere while she hiked over to Claire's room and conducted her own more focused and purposeful investigation. Knowing her as I do, she would never dismiss our contributions, but I could see that she regarded her activity as the more vital.

"Bear with me for a moment and I'll lay out for you what I suddenly realized. We had been looking outward for evidence about Claire's demise, disregarding, or actually overlooking, what she might be able to tell us. I know, I know, you'll shake your head and wonder if I've gone off my rocker. She's gone; she's not here; how can she tell us anything? Well, Claire was a fastidious person, particularly about noting her own routine and activities. Because of her vision handicap, one would not expect her to write down thoughts and schedules. But, guess what! I know for a fact, and simply forgot to look into it, that she taped her calendar of events onto a small cassette recorder she carried in her purse. So, I went in again and was rewarded with even more than I expected."

"Aha," I say with mock resolution, "she named her killer!"

"Nothing so mundane—or, in our situation, so conclusive. She likely had no way of knowing who was deliberately poisoning her. But, aside from her appointments and daily planning, she used the tape recorder to express her creative bents. Claire loved to write, mostly poetry."

"Yes!" Meredith almost explodes. "I have a dozen of her poems. She was timid about showing them off, but I insisted, and, a few months ago, she told me she would have Kinkos-FedEx transcribe her tapes and print them out for me."

"If you can produce those for us, we may have even more clues. But the ones that struck me the most were those about her sense of sisterhood with other women. Let me play you one and you'll see."

Char has already set the tiny tape in the cassette, and pushes the "play" button. Claire's voice, muscular, yet tender, broadcasts clearly her verses. Tears form in Meredith's eyes; I find them swelling in mine as well.

"We rise—or fall—in harmony,
passions haltered
by fiats from afar.

You are woman, they disparage,
partnered with man; unnatural
to crave a heart of your kind;
evil to love another like you.
Ah, how can love be evil?
how kisses contaminate?
how affection pollute?
I am old, yet fires burn,
I am old, and young at heart,
Second chances shine;
I am woman with woman!"

We sit in silence as Charlotte switched off the tape recorder. At last, Meredith says, "I don't believe she gave me that poem. All I can imagine is that she must have felt connected with her own woman-hood, and it's wonderful if she had a sense of loving again."

"Loving again," Charlotte says. "Yes. It could well mean that our elegant, dear Claire was feeling love. However, if you listen carefully at the language in her poem, and zero in on what I'm driving at, it isn't in the abstract. It is most certainly in the particular."

"You mean," I say, "that she had...well, a girlfriend?"

"Exactly what I mean. Which raises some crucial questions: who could it be, and what, if any, impact did that have on her death?"

She gets that *Charlotte look* again, as if she is off in the stars some-where, and adds, "Note that she uses the phrase 'second chances,' which could, with some stretch of the imagination, mean she has united with the same woman as before—or not. But if it is the same woman, damn it all, which one here at Bigelow is this mystery lover? Is she the reunited partner from California, who, after a long hiatus, decided to relocate to this area, or had she perhaps moved to another state, grown lonely, and wanted to test the waters again with her for-mer girlfriend? If either of these is so, how long has she been living here, and how can we track her down?"

As seems the case in this investigation, each new insight creates even more question marks. I am a bit surprised by all the questions Charlotte raises, since, usually, she's the one providing the answers. I certainly have none.

Meredith seems terribly solemn, and I can only think that she wonders how her grandmother could have been in a love relationship with another woman without Meredith's knowledge.

All I can think of to say is, "My money is on you, Char. If anyone can find her, you can."

18

I BEGIN TO think of the Bigelow population in a different light. It is highly possible that one of these women is a transplant from California, where Claire lived before entering the Village. Not only a transplant, but perhaps the woman Claire was partnered with for twenty years. Meredith had said that the two broke up when Claire became blind, and one can presume there was resentment. Had a reunion occurred? Had Claire again been stirred by the same old love?

Charlotte, more focused than I, decides to check at the desk for information about the latest move-ins—not in the last month or even six months, but in the last year.

Though she is aware of many of the new residents, it hasn't been on her agenda to systematically canvass new arrivals, and, obviously, she had never seen Claire spending inordinate amounts of time with any specific woman.

Detective Hartunian, meanwhile, is true to his word, and a broad-shouldered, squarely built, dark-haired, dark-eyed, dark-skinned, and austerely attractive woman appears on the scene. She is dressed in a tan skirt, colorful patterned blouse decorated with fleurs-de-lis, and a grey, woolen, long-sleeved sweater, open in front.

She introduces herself simply as Toni and says, "Pleased to meet you."

From that moment on, for the rest of the day, and as far as I can tell, except when Charlotte is in her apartment, Toni is never out of eyesight. I'm not sure if she carries a weapon, since she is a buxom woman and has a lot of flesh, in the folds of which she could easily hide something.

I smile as I see Freda amble from the library, cross through the lobby area, and stare curiously at this odd stranger hanging about. Does she know? Can she tell? This retirement home has so few dark-skinned people, it would be clear that this entry is an outsider.

Brenda, the desk clerk, sometimes rather aloof, is most coopera-tive, and lists for Charlotte twelve new women and six new men as starting residents in Bigelow within the last year. As soon as she gets the names, Charlotte sits in her apartment with Meredith and me (Toni is downstairs in the little waiting area close to the elevator), and begins to ruminate out loud.

"I know eleven of these eighteen names. Of the twelve women, I know nine, and I'm pretty sure none of them could be Claire's lover, so only three are strangers. Those three are, according to Brenda's information, from Massachusetts, Illinois and Colorado. What we have no way of knowing is where they lived before that, because there is no reason to believe that Claire's ex stayed in California. Aside from all that, I am beginning to doubt that any one of these new people could be Claire's renewed love."

"Why is that?" I ask.

"As far as I can tell," Charlotte says, "Claire's behavior did not change over the past year. She didn't suddenly perk up and become more excited about life. Which leads me to assume that she may have been involved with a lover for longer than any of us knew, involved secretly, and perhaps intermittently, showing no outward signs of un-usual joy."

She pauses, but only briefly. "That doesn't mean one of the arri-vals over the past year or so could not have been Claire's former love, but it could mean that the woman, whoever she is, wanted a renewal and was spurned, spurned because Claire already had someone."

"If she did have a long-term lover, she certainly hid it from me," Meredith says. "But with everything I'm finding out about her, this one more thing doesn't surprise me."

"Nor me," Charlotte says. "We all know what a private person Claire was. But—and this is the key element—something about her se-cret lover could well be at the bottom of all this. I mean, bitterness could have burgeoned, someone else could have known and taken umbrage, or, for all we know, it could have been a ménage-a-trois. Now, before we leap onto this as the ultimate *truth*, we need to entertain the possibility that some entirely different motive was occurring."

"Okay," I put in, "so what would that be?"

"We already know that Claire was resented by some for her spiritual beliefs–or lack thereof. We also know that homophobia is rampant, whether one shows affection in public or not. It may not have been any open display with another woman that set someone off, but a deep-seated fear of what might be perceived as a faulty, and, if it gets into religion, a sacrilegious sexual orientation. Hatred is often a byproduct of prejudice."

"So, the tape gives us possibilities, but does not point in any specific direction," I muse.

"I'm afraid that's about it," Charlotte muses back. "I think we know that Claire was involved with someone, but we don't know who. And, as for the more recent Village arrivals, I don't want to dismiss them completely, because there is one, Lenore Flores, whom I barely know. Though she doesn't leap out as Claire's former partner, Lenore did seem to want to be friendly with her."

She stops, and as if a new little jewel has suddenly popped in, and says, "I wonder if anyone–I mean *any*one–has shown either remorse or satisfaction over Claire's death. That is our next task: to peruse the population here at Bigelow for any shows of strong emotion."

In my need to contribute to Charlotte's creative analyses, I suggest, "It could be that one of the old-timers, a woman who has lived here for several years, is Claire's one-time partner, followed her here, and was in the shadows. Claire obviously would have known, since, even without vision, the word would have gotten around. And, if it is Lenore Flores, wouldn't you have seen some open display of emotion between them?"

"The tape implies renewal," Charlotte says, "and you seem to infer that this other woman approached Claire with hopes for a reconciliation."

"Hmm…I don't know," I reply. "But, if she is here, and did want to reunite, and still harbored resentment–well, she could be the killer. Of course, that would mean someone else is the woman on the tape."

"Yes," Meredith inserts, "a threesome is an awkward situation and could certainly result in hostile behavior."

"All of this is conjecture. Good possibilities, but nothing firm.

The gathering on the day after tomorrow will bring together the several principals, perhaps including some we don't yet know about. My expectation is that something illuminating will come out of it."

Charlotte's wall phone rings and she answers. "Oh? That would be fine. Tell her to come on up." She returns the receiver to its charge cradle, turns to us, begins to chuckle, and says, "That was Toni. Obviously, her cover is blown, since Freda approached her and asked permission to come up to my apartment. She has something important to tell us."

Freda is an impressive woman, was once what people would have considered pretty, and, as an older person, remains attractive. Despite her sharp tongue and tendency to butt-in, she is clearly bright and aware. I can't say I like her, but I feel a certain spectrum of respect.

"I know what's going on," Freda says. "I mean with the police and all."

Charlotte points to the sofa, and we all arrange ourselves in a circle so we can see and hear what Freda is about to deliver.

"Claire had enemies. A lot of it was her attitude: blind people think they deserve better treatment. Some of it was her sexual stuff: she didn't flaunt it, but everyone knew. And the rest of it was her atheism: though she wasn't openly critical of believers, she had private disdain."

She pauses and looks at each of us for some reaction. So far, everything she's revealed is already known to us, but it is unnerving to hear it expressed from someone else—and so bluntly from a person outside our little group.

"Cops can only mean crime," she continues, "so it's obvious that Claire's death was not the usual old-person-fading-away scenario. Somebody did something to Claire—and I have a pretty good guess who."

The three of us look at each other with what can only be described as surprise. Will this huffy old gal give us on a silver platter what we've been scratching for these last five days? Or is she a wonderfully clever perpetrator deliberately trying to steer us off track?

"Go on, Freda," Charlotte says evenly. I catch on her face an intense look, one I read as skepticism, but with an open mind, which she seems always to maintain.

"I've been talking around," Freda says, "and one thing I learned is that the Jew lady, Esther Hahn—the one with the vegetable husband—had a mountain of resentment against Claire. In her case, it had to do with religion. She's a dogmatic old bitch, disappears on Saturday, hates the Christmas celebrations here at Bigelow, won't ride on the Sabbath, won't turn the TV on or off on Friday night.

"Now there is an example of hypocrisy, since she isn't supposed to even ask someone else to do it for her; but she once invited a non-Jewish woman in and kept pointing at the TV until the other person got the message—and, since then, someone has been doing it for her every week. To me that is pure horseshit, and a violation of the essence of her rigid beliefs."

In as kind a way as she can, Charlotte says, "You know, Freda, insulting a person's spiritual rituals is not what you came to do. Surely you have some important information we can use?"

"Yes, well, I spoke with Esther in a deep way earlier today, and here's what she said. She said, 'Claire deserved what she got,' and she said, 'People can't live the kind of Godless life she lived and turn out all right.' Then she almost growled at me as she finished up with, 'The wicked die alone.'"

When she says this, I think of the Broadway musical, *Wicked*, and the song containing those exact lyrics. At once, I wonder if Freda is gaming us, making this all up, trying to throw us off the scent. After all, at the memorial service, Esther did come up to Charlotte and the rest of us afterward and say how important it was for people to live and let live.

"So, all this vitriol coming from Esther leads you to the conclusion that she may have done something to hurt Claire?" Charlotte asks.

"Sure, but along with that, there is one other thing."

"What is that?" Meredith asks.

Freda rises, circles the room, stops for a moment by the window, and begins to massage her left shoulder. She turns and slowly retreats to her seat, now rubbing her left forearm. A look in her eyes seems to broadcast that she is struggling with some sort of chronic pain.

"I suffer from fibromyalgia, and have been taking St. John's wort to help with the pain. It's supposed to be a natural element and not a very common supplement, but has to be used carefully with other meds. I recall once mentioning it to that old, inflexible bitch. I mean, it's nothing to hide. A few weeks ago, I discovered my supply had been stolen from my purse. Today, when I was questioning Esther, she opened her purse for a tissue, and guess what? I saw in there a plastic bottle of St. John's wort. It had to be mine."

19

I AM IMPRESSED that Charlotte's apartment looks cleanly bright and I wonder if she does her own housekeeping. I do, at my home in California, and I'm afraid my place reflects a disinterested attitude. I'm not dirty and I hate clutter, but I don't vacuum or dust as often as required for my home to match my sister's.

When Freda has departed from this bright and clean apartment, Charlotte waits some thirty seconds, then breaks into laughter.

"What?" I say.

"What's funny?" Meredith asks.

"She is—a real kick in the ass. First of all, we know St. John's wort, when carelessly combined with other meds, can be toxic. And we already are aware that Freda has fibromyalgia. What is highly unlikely is that Esther Hahn—the Jew lady, as Freda, the bigot, calls her—ever had access to Claire's rooms. They were not friends—well, I don't think Freda and Claire were either—and I never saw Esther so much as approach Claire, let alone visit her. Her husband, yes, out of dementia-innocence, but only in the dining hall."

Meredith paces, and wears a worried look. "I'm really getting frustrated. Every possible lead has holes in it. Surely, that ugly language Esther used—at least according to Freda—means something."

"Yes," Charlotte says instantly, "it means that the first part of Freda's testimony is accurate: Claire was her own person, and a lot of people were put off by it."

"Freda is a smart cookie," I say. "What about the possibility that she is deliberately trying to deflect? I mean why couldn't she have been the one slipping the St. John's wort into the wrong pill bottles?"

"It's possible. She's ornery enough to do anything. But, my sense of it is that Freda is too confrontational to sneak around altering labels and writing threatening notes. Whenever she appreciates or rejects what's going on, she makes it known, loudly and clearly."

"In that way," I put in, "she reminds me of our mom, especially in her later years. Old Lilah Smart was blunt and opinionated. I have pictures of her on my mantel, photographs where she looks matronly and pleasant, but still foreboding. I'm sure you remember her that way."

"She resented me," Charlotte says. "I came on the scene when she was trying to finish her college degree, which she was forced to postpone. You were her favorite, the golden boy of her last few fecund years."

"Sorry," I say to Meredith, who seems impatient. "Didn't mean to tangent off into ancient history."

"Yes," Charlotte says, "but what you were saying may have clarified one thing. Freda's own family experience could have contributed to her becoming a curmudgeon, but it also helps illuminate the fact that a lot of these elder statesmen—and women—are fixed in cement when it comes to tolerance. They are all products of their ancient history; change is painful and hard to come by."

"That leaves us with a smorgasbord of possibilities," Meredith says, despondently. "Any one of a couple hundred residents could have mustered up the gumption to strike out against what offended them."

"It isn't as dismal as all that," Charlotte says. "I'd say we've narrowed it down to a dozen or so Bigelow people and maybe half a dozen outsiders."

"Does Hartunian know that?" I ask.

My comment brings more laughter from my insightful sister. "Dear brother, I'm afraid that sweet, but naïve, Detective Hartunian, at least at this point, doesn't know much."

—

It doesn't snow. But it does turn frigid. A dry, icy blast circles down from the Great Lakes, and I see that the temperature drop adds to Meredith's despair.

Toni, the "outed" policewoman, informs us at 8:00 PM that she will be going home, but she cautions Charlotte. "Stay indoors. I'll return tomorrow morning at eight."

Toni has a pleasing way about her, and I wonder what steers a woman into law enforcement. Would have been an interesting question to ask Claire. Perhaps Meredith knows the answer.

Generously, Meredith tells Charlotte she will sleep over again in her apartment, though I believe it is partly for herself; being alone in this charged environment cannot be very comforting.

Before Toni can get away, I ask her if she will drop me off at my motel, and with a pleasant smile, she says, "I will do that."

As we are leaving, Charlotte says, "Why don't you stay in the guest apartment tonight? Tomorrow morning, I want to make another tour of Claire's apartment. If she has composed poetry and made tapes for a woman she cherished, we might presume that she received something in return. You're welcome to join me."

I agree, and thank Toni. A lot more comfortable to avoid the freezing weather and bed down in a warm room close at hand. Besides, it will keep me near my sister should anything strange happen.

Charlotte rings Brenda at the front desk, and leaves a message that I will be staying for another night, noting that I still have the room key.

Most of the population of the Village retires early, and the long halls at night are deserted and spooky. It's not that I'm frightened, but I can see where it is easy to do mischief in a place where, considering that all the inhabitants are elderly, activity slows to a halt in the dark.

It is inky dark—and it is windy and terribly cold. The lobbies and dining hall and meeting rooms are heated, but the passageways are not, and the north wind steals its way through cracks and under doors, so that by the time I reach my rented apartment I am chilled.

A few yards from my room is an indoor atrium where white rattan chairs with flowery cushions are set around a glass coffee table. To my surprise, a man is seated there, reading.

Enter Romeo.

He grins as I pass, and says in a cheerful voice, "Nippy, isn't it?"

It must be for him, certainly, since, over his basic clothing, he is wearing only a light, pale blue, woolen sweater. The rest of his attire, linen slacks and white Florsheim shoes, is elegant, almost out-of-place in a retirement village, where most residents barely make it financially, and certainly dress economically.

I am to learn in the next day or two that, yes, he comes from money, and his actual name is Romano, but, because he has a penchant for flirting with the Village women, has been dubbed Romeo. He is not rotund, but has an ample belly, is of moderate height, wears a constant smile, and, most strikingly, has a head of pure white hair and a full white beard. Santa Claus in the flesh—and he appears to be about my sister's age.

"Sure is," I say. "You must be freezing, sitting there."

"I'm used to it. Grew up in Newfoundland. I'm a Newfy!"

"Well, I'm from California. I'm afraid my blood is thin."

"That's a myth, you know. Blood doesn't thin in warm climates. It's what you're used to."

"Uh…I guess that's true."

"You're Charlotte's brother."

"I am. Visiting."

"I heard you speak last year. You wouldn't recognize me. Had no facial hair then. Enjoyed your pitch. We elder guys get bogged down in routine. Lots of folks here get stuck, like deeply rooted trees. They need new ideas. Need variety. I guess I'm somewhat different from the crowd."

"Yes. Well, I don't mean this as an insult in any way, but you look different. Kind of appealing, actually, but certainly unique. I don't know any other Newfy gents, but I doubt they all look like you."

I am magnetized by his robust laugh, as he replies, "Not a one. That's the beauty of being a trendsetter rather than a follower. No one dictates to me. I do what I like, when I like."

"Okay. I can see that. So, don't mean to be discourteous, but I'm going to turn in now."

As if I had said nothing, he continues, "We all need variety. In food, in friends, and, for us old guys, variety in women." His hearty laugh comes again, and I find myself liking him, despite his penchant for self-compliments.

I nod and put my key in the lock, as thoughts rummage through me about this possible new candidate in Claire's demise. After all, Charlotte keeps encouraging us to keep an open mind since anyone could have some sort of hidden agenda we know nothing about.

"Good night," I say over my shoulder.

"Charlotte is a handsome lady," Romeo says. He rises and strolls away.

20

THOUGH CHARLOTTE describes him as naïve, Hartunian isn't a nerd. I presume he has been doing some investigating and that he, as well as Charlotte, has some leads. So far, what I have observed is that he lacks my sister's intuitive sense. For him, it's an imperfect science; for Charlotte, it's an art.

The next morning, Meredith and share a breakfast of oatmeal and raisins, along with coffee for me and tea for her, in Charlotte's apartment.

"Detective Hartunian called at seven-thirty this morning," Charlotte says. "It seems Freda bent his ear at the memorial, and now he is hot on the trail of Esther Hahn. I tried to disencumber him of that notion, tried to pry him loose from galloping off in that direction, but it didn't work. He talked as if *truth* had suddenly descended upon him, and he was compelled to pursue it."

"Kind of an unbending personality, if you ask me," Meredith puts out, wiping her soft lips with a red, linen napkin.

"Yep," I add, "and though he is a professional, he reacts in an impetuous way, more like a rank amateur."

"Now, now," Charlotte says, wiping her lips with a blue linen napkin, "don't write the man off. He's a bit too desperate to solve this crime—could be a big deal for him in this backwoods precinct. But, I believe he is quicker than he has shown. After we've examined Claire's apartment, I want to consult with him."

"Yes, and I'll bet he wants to consult with you," I say, wiping my lips with a green linen napkin.

We are quiet for a moment, and I say, "Elegant napkins, Sis. You really know how to coddle your guests."

—

Toni, our intrepid protector, greets us as we exit the elevator en route for Claire's apartment.

"Morning, folks. I trust you had a peaceful night."

"Your boss called," Charlotte informs her. "Wants you to know he's following up on a few leads."

Toni smiles a full, welcoming smile, her paper-white teeth a bold contrast with her very dark skin, and says, "I'll be like a shadow on the wall—out of your way, but never out of your sight."

"Good," I say.

"We're going to the intensive care wing," Charlotte says, "so if you want, you can shadow us there."

Out of earshot, Charlotte tells Meredith and me, "Toni's presence is overkill in a way. I doubt that the person we're looking for would get openly violent, threats or not. Acts of violence would bring too much attention. Our perp did something subtle, and almost—but, as I hope to prove in the not-too-distant future—not quite undetectable."

"But bad guys do get violent when backed into a corner," I say. "The closer we come to an identification, the more desperate the person will become."

"He or she already erred in writing those notes, since it broadcast to the world that a crime occurred. In their desperation, law breakers, while often shrewd, are also prone to carelessness. My guess is that our culprit in this little escapade, to avoid making any more flagrant mistakes, will attempt to lie low and fade into the shadows."

"Still," Meredith says, "I do feel more protected with Toni around."

I glance quickly at Meredith, feeling helpless with love. How deeply I want her safety, as well as Charlotte's!

Claire's apartment is like a refrigerator, the heat having been turned off for over a week. I wonder if we are going to explore randomly, or if Charlotte has a plan. My unspoken question is answered at once.

Ignoring the cold and the weird feeling of emptiness, Charlotte, quite businesslike, says, "The two of you—why don't you examine all the tapes on those shelves, both audio and video. I'll go through the drawers and cubbyholes in her desk, and I also want to rifle through her closet just a bit."

There are some thirty CDs on the shelves, at least a dozen cassettes, and only three videotapes. It makes sense that Claire wouldn't watch videos, unless someone was with her, adding to the dialogue with narrative about the scenes. Each tape is labeled in braille, appliqués over the original titles. I heard Charlotte once say that Claire was able to purchase tapes with braille transcripts accompanying them. It was one way she entertained herself.

I keep looking over at Charlotte to see how she's doing; Claire's rooms, aside from being cold, are barren, devoid of life. No newspapers or magazines, no music or voices, the kitchen empty of food, the refrigerator disconnected and silent. It is both eerie and depressing.

After a few minutes, as she shuts the closet door, Charlotte asks, "Find anything useful?"

"Not sure," Meredith answers. "There are a couple of cassettes bearing initials. I doubt that Grandmother would have written initials she couldn't see, so it means they are from someone else."

"Yes, someone else who either didn't know or didn't care that Claire couldn't read them," I add.

"Let's take them with us and we'll play them. By the way, in the kitchen trash basket is a crumpled pastry box with Wally Burt's café logo on it; confirms that he has visited. Meanwhile, I found something significant, though I'm afraid we may need Hartunian and his forensics people to help us."

Same as last time we were in Claire's place, I notice that Charlotte has slipped on plastic gloves. In her right hand, distinctive against the pink of her glove, is a yellow piece of paper about four inches by six inches. Typical of her, there is also something in her left hand—a bluish paper, which, not in a clandestine way but without fanfare or a mention, she casually slides into her pocket. I already know not to ask about such things. She seems to know exactly the timeframe for disclosing information to Meredith and me.

She holds up the yellow paper, gives us both an intense look, and reads its words aloud. "'LEAVE HER ALONE!' It's printed in the style of the threatening notes to me."

—

Charlotte reasons that the note has to do with the person we believe had a romance with Claire, and that someone, very likely the killer, perhaps a homophobe, possibly a bigot, was angry about it. We ask Toni to phone her boss and request he meet us at noon. Since the wind and temperature are so severe, I agree enthusiastically when Meredith suggests we don't go out, but instead that Hartunian come to Bigelow. I volunteer my rented apartment, since I have tenaciously clung to the key and since Brenda hasn't demanded it. The Blue Dolphin harbors my suitcase and most of my toiletries, and, in some convoluted way, I miss it. I've always been that way. Though it may seem rather ludicrous, hotel rooms–with their firm beds, fresh towels, personal soap bars, and daily maid service–appeal to me.

Charlotte picks up the cassette player from her residence, and we meet in my place, snacking on Hershey's Kisses, waiting for Hartunian. I'm a chocolate nut, and, with the new evidence that dark chocolate is full of antioxidants, I often overdo it. Seldom a day passes in which I don't consume chocolate in some form: cocoa, ice cream, candy bars, milkshakes, and the portable Hershey's Kisses. I always stock up at the Times Square Hershey's retail shop whenever I take the train in to visit Charlotte.

"It's good," Meredith says, "but wickedly fattening."

"Everything in moderation," Charlotte, on her fourth kiss, replies.

"Does that go for romance?" I ask, sneaking a glance at Meredith.

"I'd say," Charlotte laughs, "that considering what we're dealing with, an overdose of most things ought to be avoided. But, I'm willing to make an exception when it comes to love."

"Me too," Meredith says, without looking at me.

"Me three," I say, trying hard not to look at her.

There is a quiet moment and I toss out, "Who is Santa Claus?"

My quick sister answers immediately, "You must be asking about Jerry Romano, or Romeo, as he is known hereabouts."

"Yeah. He was sitting outside my door last night. Amiable fellow, but with some kind of agenda."

"I'm sure," Charlotte says. "It's almost always the same agenda, and, even though these folks are all in the latter stages of life, he seems intent on trying to persuade some woman, hopefully one who is ambulatory and with all her senses, to accompany him back to his room."

"A devout romantic," Meredith says, "and with romance, age doesn't matter."

"Yes!" I respond. "Age doesn't matter."

"Well, but Romano always seems to hit on the slightly younger residents."

"He was complimentary about you."

"Because, and you'll pardon my language, he'd like to get into my pants."

"Charlotte!" Meredith blurts out, with a grin.

"What? I like to think of myself as a modern woman."

"You are, you are," Meredith says.

"So," I ask, bringing us back to Romano, "did this Santa dude know Claire? Could he be a possible suspect? I mean, if Claire rejected his advances?"

"Not too farfetched," Charlotte says. "But, with her blindness and all, I doubt Romano would have hit on Claire. He's after women who are hale and hearty."

With a laugh, I say, "You know, Sis, it wouldn't hurt for you to give him a tumble."

"You mean it wouldn't hurt *you*," she replies, quick-witted as always.

—

A different Hartunian enters in the next half hour, and asks Toni to join him in my apartment. I say different because, for some unspoken reason, he seems to want to dominate our group, a little Napoleon, governing his troops. Only we aren't soldiers, and he hasn't been designated our leader.

I see that my sister is amused, lips in a bit of a pout, a merry twinkle in her eyes. She listens avidly to his pitch.

"Okay, lovely people, now listen up. This investigation has been stalled, and partly because of interference from all of you. I know you mean well, but your trespasses have likely caused the perp to go underground and cover his trail even more."

"Now, Augie, we really have not trespassed. We are connected to the victim and are simply trying to understand what happened."

"Yeah, but our office has been trying to follow up on the forensics and have made a little progress. We need to set a trap for the suspect—whoever that may be—and catch him or her in the act. I say *in the act* because criminals almost always repeat themselves, sometimes for protection when law enforcement gets too close, and sometimes because a witness surfaces who can finger them…"

His message begins to be obvious, and Charlotte interrupts.

"Yes, of course, Detective Hartunian, and we shall certainly co-operate. Now here is another bit of evidence your lab people can check out. We found this in the victim's apartment. It was not fingered by any of us, so any prints might provide valuable information."

She produces the yellow paper, now in a plastic baggie, and hands it to Hartunian, who, when he reads the words, says, "Aha!"

I can almost not contain myself, since he seems a lot like the bumbling movie detective, Inspector Clouseau, of *Pink Panther* fame.

"And by the way," Charlotte adds, "tomorrow's assembly of merchants and eager shoppers will bring together most, if not all, of the possible suspects. We can certainly look upon that gathering as the 'trap' you refer to."

"Hmm, you're right," a more subdued Hartunian says. Then, still holding to the program planted in him through his conversation with Freda, he asks, "Will that Esther woman be there?"

"Oh yes, she is a dedicated shopper at these merchant fairs. What I propose," Charlotte tacks on, "is that at an appropriate time, we ask the top dozen likely suspects to take a break from their enterprise, and join us in a little 'private tribute' to Claire, in her apartment. We'll have candles lit, and a cassette player with some of Claire's favorite music playing. Neither innocent nor guilty can set aside curiosity. If my hunch is anywhere near accurate, the criminal will, hopefully, be unmasked."

"What, little lady, is your hunch?"

"Oh, I don't want to say at this moment. It would be unfair to point the finger prematurely."

The detective looks confused. Toni, more alert than her boss, grins at all of us, and says, "You are one crafty woman. If you need anything from me, let me know. I can't wait till tomorrow."

Hartunian frowns at his aide, but says lamely, "Yeah, of course."

—

"I don't expect anything from the note," Charlotte says. The three of us are alone in my apartment, Toni and Hartunian having retreated to their respective duties.

"There will be no prints because the killer is at least clever enough to wipe them off or wear gloves. I would, however, welcome news from Hartunian about any anomalies in the pill containers.

Again, I doubt that there will be, but it is possible that at one point, the person slipped up, got careless, and made one of those crucial mistakes I mentioned."

"I'm wondering," I say, "about the headaches Claire was getting before she was killed. You mentioned that serotonin syndrome can cause a stroke, but would the headaches be a precursor? Like a warning sign?"

"She told me she had headaches," Meredith says. "I didn't get alarmed because many people get them, and they don't lead to anything more serious."

"You got it, Greg. The research I did noted that excessive serotonin in the brain can cause several symptoms, including dizziness and headache...and ultimately, stroke."

She holds up the small cassette player. "Let's see what these audio tapes have contain."

The first one is a classical rendition of Cole Porter's "I've Got You Under My Skin," by Frank Sinatra, one of Claire's favorite entertainers.

"A love song," Meredith says.

We play the second tape, "You'll Never Walk Alone," from the musical *Carousel*.

"A song of community," I say.

"From one lover to another," Charlotte adds.

21

I WANDER OVER to the auditorium where workmen are setting up two-dozen long tables covered with white butcher paper. The merchant event brings in no revenue to Bigelow, so it is an act of generosity and a public relations move for them to accommodate the numerous community vendors. As I view it, an attempt is made to keep expenses down, and there are no decorations or signposts.

Charlotte's apartment serves as our headquarters during this troubling time, and I return there to hear her voice within. Cautioned not to keep her door unlocked, she opens it at my call, with the small phone to her ear.

I hear her say, "Yes, dear, so I need to talk privately with you once you have a free moment. After your table is set up, of course."

Upon returning her phone to its cradle, Charlotte spins around with a smile. "Good old Wally. Such a lovely person."

"Obviously not a suspect," I say.

"Well…as the gendarmes like to say, 'Everyone is a suspect!' but Wally is less of a suspect than most."

"I guess Meredith had to go into work."

"She'll be back later in the afternoon. Another dear person. I am so glad to finally get to know her. Our Claire was indeed fortunate to have a granddaughter like her."

Her words sting me—not because I disagree, but because I agree too much. She is a dear person, and a sweetheart, but not mine. There is a song in the Broadway musical, *Wicked,* about a boy who gets a girlfriend, to which the singer laments, "I'm not that girl." Though it tears at my heart, where Meredith is concerned, I'm clearly not that boy.

The strong wind backs off, yet the sun struggles to push any warmth onto the Pennsylvania countryside. I decide to bundle up (Charlotte has a down jacket that fits me) and take a solitary walk in the neighborhood, the fall hues almost gone, the multi-colored leaves skittering noisily in the light breeze, along the paved roads and gently sloping dunes.

Toni sees me leaving the complex and says, "Brenda, the desk clerk, sort of coolly asked if she could help me. I'm afraid I lied. I told her I worked for a national research group and we were studying the treatment of the elderly in selected retirement homes. After that, I observed her attitude and it seemed much more pleasant. I heard her say, with a smile, 'How can I help you, dearie?' to one woman, and, 'My, you look lovely today,' to another."

"Good for you, Toni. Be sure to give Bigelow Village high marks in your report."

Few autos circle into the grounds of the Village, and my walk is marked by a soothing aloneness, although, off and on, a chattering squirrel, darker in color than those near my California home, whips its tail and scrambles up a tree, perhaps startled by a tall creature foolish enough to be strolling about in thirty-five-degree weather.

I really would like to clear my head about Meredith. The pursuit of Claire's killer is primarily in Charlotte's hands, and, of course, questionable as they may be, the professional law-enforcement hands of the august Augustus Hartunian. So, there isn't much for me to do in that serious arena. Meredith, however, is another ball of wax. I mean, no one can solve the conundrum of her position as opposed to mine. She remains wounded from the loss of an intense love, and, it seems, is not open to considering someone new. Or, perhaps, though it hurts me deeply to contemplate, she is not open to considering *me*.

I pass a thick grove of fir trees and hear movement deep within, perhaps another animal, or maybe one chasing one. That universal need, the built-in drive for companionship. All animals crave company. Humans, particularly, are social beings. But, even more, we are seekers of intimacy. Pair-bonding, which started thousands of years ago and evolved into something we now call marriage, has never gone out of style, even in the United States, where the divorce rate for first marriages exceed fifty percent (and is higher still among those who remarry).

My brain turns the problem over and over. I've stopped my walk without really being aware of it.

It is not so odd for me to want to nest with someone, especially someone as appealing as Meredith Hazelton. She is damned beautiful. She is smart. There is tenderness about her, softness, an extraordinary depth that pulls me in. Her life is exquisitely organized. Her life, alas, is her own.

I must resolve to let go. She won't come my way. I punish myself with my obsession. Unrequited, one-way love is too painful to pursue, day after day, week after week. And given the geography of our situation, how foolish I've been, stupid really, to have clung to this false hope. I was right.

Two squirrels send the leaves flying as they leap out of the forest. They scramble away and, in the dead silence that follows, I hear the gurgle of water somewhere in the forest. I decide to climb in and investigate. Sure enough, after about a hundred feet of maneuvering around the barrels of several dozen trees, the land slopes down to a tumbling little creek, almost, but not quite frozen. Musical, the splash of the leaping water, and I listen for emerging patterns, for a melody, so I can apply lyrics.

Ta-plink, ta-plink. ta-plink, the rhythm, constant the meter, and my mind hears, *too late, too late, too late.* Aloud I say, "To win the love of my life."

How dumb of me! This heavenly spot on the planet, pristine, bubbling over with the perfume of life–and I defile it with "poor-me" whining.

I begin to ponder *if only* thoughts in a desperation that leaves me feeling pitiful. Yet, I suppose we all have an inner core that pushes us toward survival, because, in the next moment, I am saying to the creek, "I'm a good person. There has to be someone who will love me. Painful as it is, I must move on. There are, as the guys say in California, 'oodles of poodles' out there. One will surely have my name on it–on her!"

As if my words are magnets, a pair of geese waddle down the opposite slope, cross the stream, and begin, slowly, with a certain caution, to pick their way toward me, perhaps expecting to be fed.

Remembering Charlotte's description of the wild geese contaminating the local area, I wave my arms and shout, "Shoo!" They flap their wings, squawk at me ferociously, as if scolding, and clumsily leap away.

Feelings ruffled, mood dark, I turn and pick my way back through the trees to the path at the edge of the road. Cold as it is, with my down jacket I feel as if I am in a tent, snug and protected, hands with gloves, head in the parka, neck wrapped in a woolen scarf.

I move on for perhaps a hundred yards, alone with thoughts bordering on despair, and finally slide down to the ground just at the side of the road, with my knees up and my back at the base of a thick tree that I think is a cedar. I sit and wonder, sit and reminisce. I ponder the myriad possibilities a life can experience, routes we select, tangents that whimsically propel us wide of our desired marks.

And tears come.

For several stretched minutes I remain this way, strong in many ways, weak in many others.

A car rolls up the Bigelow road. I try to ignore it, but the driver, after passing me, suddenly applies the breaks, stops abruptly, slips into reverse, and backs up to my spot.

I raise my eyes as the passenger door swings open, and see, leaning across, a worried look fouling her lovely countenance, the object of my discontent, Meredith Hazelton.

"You look lost," she says. "Come on, get in."

The car heater is on. I sink down in the passenger seat, feeling both warm and embarrassed. Meredith drives forward to the edge of the buildings, pulls her car into a parking slot (reminding me of how I stole hers when we first met), switches off the motor and turns toward me.

"What's up?" she asks.

"I'm a shithead."

"Besides that?"

"Oh, you don't want to know," I say.

"I wouldn't ask if I didn't want to know."

"Look, Meredith, every now and then I get to feeling sorry for myself."

"Go on."

"It's stupid. I have a perfectly functional life."

"But…"

"But…I don't know. It feels…*I feel* empty."

"I suppose we all feel that way at different times, Greg. But you sound as if this is chronic."

"The West Coast, my life there, is challenging: I have friends, entertainment is plentiful, my living quarters are comfortable, meals are satisfying, I exercise regularly, I sleep soundly, and…I suffer." I sigh with this admission.

Meredith's penetrating emerald eyes stare at me, a look of both empathy and curiosity. "The bottom line, Greg. Suffer from…?"

"It's dumb. I mean, I don't want to come across as self-pitying. So many people have it worse."

"I've learned never to compare suffering. What makes you unhappy is critical for you."

"Okay, Meredith. But, I still feel as if I ought not to be complaining."

"That's another story. How you express your misery is your choice, and complaining only works if the listener can make a difference."

"Ah, you've hit it. *Can* the listener make a difference?"

She seems, suddenly and with a reddening of her cheeks, to get it. She is silent for several seconds until softly saying, "You want something from me."

I am quiet as well, and finally answer, also softly, "I do."

I know about self-centeredness; I see people where I teach who are "me, me, me" afflicted, perhaps, in a psychological sense, aptly labeled narcissistic. But I've never considered myself in that category. Now, with Meredith leaning toward me, so close and yet so far, I feel dysfunctional and self-focused. Without saying the words, I have sent out the message that I am relationally deprived, only half a person, and no one but she can fix me and make me whole. Even as I ponder this, I swell with disdain at my own absurdity.

"Look," Meredith says evenly, as she places a bare hand on my heavy, down sleeve, "we've skirted this long enough. I need—or I want—to tell you that no other person can ever be the antidote to your feelings of loneliness. If you make yourself miserable about your life situation, only *you* can make yourself unmiserable. You want a woman in your life? A sweetheart you can love and hold close and cherish forever? Everybody's wish! But some people do have such a partner and still drag around in despair—because the cure for loneliness is inside them."

"Do you mean…?"

She interrupts. "When it comes to relationships, no one can rescue anyone else."

I blow out air from puffed cheeks and sink even lower in my seat.

"Damn it," I say forlornly, "I know. I teach it in my classes. I try to explain that you can only be responsible for yourself. But when it's happening to me, it's a burden I find hard to bear."

She waits, those jade-like eyes focusing unwaveringly on me.

I rev up all my courage, inhale hugely, and exhale with a sudden rush of air.

"All right, Meredith. Here it is. I'm hopelessly in love with you. I see you a few days a year. We hug hello and hug goodbye. So, tell me how I can rescue myself from that one-way obsession!"

Again, she falls silent. I swear I see a tiny smile at the sides of her lips. It surely has to be flattering to know you are loved, but can also be a burden if that love is an imposition.

At last, in a soft voice she says something I don't hear, or at least don't absorb. "Who says it's one-way?"

Lost in my own world, I ramble on. "I'm not a hopeless neurotic, but I have an empty place in my heart that…"

"I do too," she interrupts. "Did you even hear what I just said?"

I pause. My memory slides back. Her words, that phrase, is it…did she say…?

"Wait a minute." I sit up straight and turn toward her. Did you just ask, 'Who says it's one-way?' Did you ask that? Is that what you meant?"

"Sure. I've had long talks with Charlotte about you. She's not only a sleuth, she's also a brilliant life coach. With her sensitive clarifying, I've come to realize…well, that I *do* love you. Now, Greg, hold on a minute. There are obstacles. I'm not a masochist. We live and work at opposite sides of a giant country. And that book by Jordan and Margaret Paul, in its title, asks a key question: *Do I Have to Give Up Me to Be Loved by You?*"

"No!" I blurt out.

"So, tell me which of us is going to cash in his or her life?"

Logic, in this charged moment, is beyond me, the practical aspect of my love for Meredith beyond comprehension. I want to devour her, smother her with affection, and hold on to her for dear life, before her revelation takes wing and forever flies off into the cold November sky.

I extend my gloved hands wide in supplication, and say, "I don't know, I don't know."

She laughs and hugs me, deliciously, though my parka is between her face and mine.

What I really don't know is whether to shout, "Thank you, Charlotte!" and surround Meredith with a show of my love–a love I've waited to extend to her for so long–or shy away and await her next move. Details aside, this is a towering moment in my life.

When she pulls away, Meredith faces me nose to nose, eyes to eyes, mouth to mouth, tips her head forward and kisses me firmly, lips to lips.

Outside, twenty feet in front of the car, beside a juvenile fir sapling, another dark brown squirrel sits up on its hind legs and chatters at us, as if scolding, "I know what you're doing!"

We exit Meredith's car and walk slowly toward the Village entrance, her right arm hooked inside my left elbow, the frigid air forgotten and the valiant sun a radiant smile on our backs.

Many relish bragging about perfect moments. Maslow referred to them as 'peak experiences.' In my life, I cannot remember any moment more vivid, more ecstatic, than this. If there were a mirror handy, I'm sure I'd see myself grinning like Alice's Cheshire Cat.

We reach the front stoop, and, as we are about to enter the exterior door to the complex, some impulse pulls my eyes upward. I see, at a second-story window, staring down at us, also grinning wildly, the white-haired, white-bearded, Romano. Romeo. Santa Claus.

22

TONI RUSHES UP to us in what appears to be crisis mode, under control and urgent at the same time. Meredith and I pull up short, stare at Toni, frozen with fear that her agitated manner concerns Charlotte.

"An old gal, the one with the cane, she collapsed. Right over there, near the counter. There was a blonde guy with her. Someone said it was her grandson. The young doc had her taken on a gurney over to the medical rooms. Said she was fragile. Said her breathing was shallow. I had to make the other residents stand back. Lots of moaning and groaning."

"What about Charlotte?" I ask, trying not to be too frantic.

"She was here. Went with the doc. They were the only two who seemed under control."

"The woman who collapsed, Trudy, you don't think there was any foul play?" Meredith asks.

"Don't know," Toni says. "She's pretty old. Looked to me like she just keeled over."

"Yes," I say to Meredith, "but is it a sequel to Claire? An accumulation of something foul?"

"Don't jump to conclusions," Meredith replies. "Trudy is cantankerous, but I don't know that anyone resented her. I think my grandmother simply rubbed somebody the wrong way."

A shroud of gloom seems to hang in the Bigelow halls, a palpable sense of distress that I imagine erupts whenever a resident becomes ill. Charlotte once mentioned that the only real negative in communal retirement living is the propinquity of illness, injury, or death. It is like a constant threat below the surface, contaminating moods, dampening the spirit of merriment.

On the carpet, near the counter where Brenda works, is Trudy's wooden cane, which no one has bothered to retrieve. A marker she left behind. I realize in this moment that we all leave markers behind.

I retrieve it and lay it on the counter top, nodding to Brenda, who seems to understand.

Seconds later, Charlotte is walking briskly toward us through the long corridor from the medical wing, face grim.

"Trudy is hanging on," she whispers, her tone guarded to keep from enflaming the residents still milling about. "It doesn't look good, at least as Overstreet sees it. I wish Doolittle were here. He's far more sympathetic. Overstreet could easily decide to give up on Trudy because she's 'so old.'"

Charlotte pauses and steps back, assessing Meredith and me with a curious scrutiny. "Something's different," she says.

How she notices is beyond me, yet I have learned not to be surprised by anything Charlotte catches.

Meredith says, "Oh, well, Greg and I had a...a breakthrough of sorts. We realize we're very fond of each other." She stops and smiles.

"That's nice," Charlotte says. "I'm fond of both of you. So, what?"

"Aw, Sis, it's a different kind of fondness. You know. A man and a woman. That sort of thing."

"Hmm, it seems pretty cerebral to me."

Meredith laughs a full, hearty laugh, and declares, "Hey, Greg and I have known each other for a few years. Don't you think that's long enough to take the surprise out of it?"

Charlotte frowns. "Listen carefully, the two of you. If you want it to last, you'd better keep the surprise in it."

Romeo Romano exits the elevator from the second floor and approaches us.

When I did my annual workshops, had he been bearded the way he now is, surely I would have noticed the full, luxurious, snow-white whiskers that sit like an overstuffed pillow on his sweatered chest.

"Haloo, Charlotte, and you two youngsters as well. Didn't see it, but heard that Trudy went down. Ah, well, every day another one falls. It's the bane of country living—or at least our kind of country living."

"Don't be vulgar, Romeo," Charlotte says. "Each of these folks is an individual whom we need to treat with respect."

He retreats at once; I see admiration for Charlotte, concession to her views. "Oh, for sure. I didn't mean to be crude in any way."

"Do you know Claire's granddaughter? This is Meredith. Meredith, Jerry Romano. You already know my brother, Greg."

"I do, I do. Hmm. Those words sound like I'm getting married."

"Not you, Jerry. You'd lose your Romeo status."

"Hey, I'm no Don Juan; I just like women, that's all. Not once, in my whole life have I ever forced myself on someone."

"I know. It's not that you're a loose lothario, it's that you don't have a stop sign. So many women, so little time."

He gives us that wide, hairy grin, and begins to sing a famous Sinatra song about the waiting game.

Esther Hahn appears around the far side of the counter, her Alzheimer husband, Elmore, in tow. Upon seeing us, she grabs Elmore's elbow and steers him to our little group.

"I think Trudy ate something rotten in the dining room and it polluted her blood," she announces. "At Trudy's age, the slightest digestive inconvenience can throw her body off."

Charlotte gives her a sharp look and says, "None of us ought to consume the wrong foods—or the wrong supplements. Look at Claire. She very well could have been poisoned from improper mixtures."

Esther's face contorts into a scowl. "She had other problems. One must keep faith with the eternal. If you go astray, you pay."

Ah, I think, an amateur poet—or at least an aficionado of rhyme.

"Certainly, Esther, but even if you like to think so, her atheism didn't kill her."

"I don't tell others what to believe but I do hold myself to the highest of standards when it comes to God."

Our little cluster falls silent and I look around at the faces. Romeo is nearly expressionless, Meredith wears a wry smile, Charlotte issues a piercing stare.

"Are you coming to the merchant fair tomorrow?" Charlotte asks.

"Wouldn't miss it. Several things I need for Elmore. Plus, the very tasty creations from New Hope, from Wally Burt's place."

"I like Wally Burt's place," Elmore puts in.

Ah, so this couple is familiar with Wally's Nutrition for The Heart-y. Might be a good idea to keep in mind that Elmore would not be inhibited from saying whatever he can remember.

Another voice cuts into our ensemble as Freda marches up and says loudly, "Hard to tell when your time will come. Anybody know if old Trudy is still hanging in there?"

"I left the medical offices a few minutes ago. She was still with us," Charlotte says in a voice of undisguised irritation.

Freda stares at Esther with contempt and mutters, "Sometimes the powers that be lean on the wrong person."

Esther grips her husband's wrist and pulls him away as she replies, "Those who turn hateful will not go unpunished."

"Damned loony bunch we have here," Meredith whispers to me.

Freda snorts and surreptitiously pumps her middle finger at the departing Esther, though because of where we are all standing, I may be the only one who sees it.

"Old folks can get as nasty as the young ones," Romano says. "I'm a peaceful person, myself. Why can't everyone just get along?"

Charlotte nods, and I can't help but wonder if good old Romeo isn't sort of putting us on. All that innocence!

Brenda, who has been leaning on the counter several feet away, but has obviously been listening to our conversation, practically shouts to be heard. "We need to clear the lobby! I have work to get done and can't do it with all these folks moping about."

I am struck, again, by the very obvious New England accent in her voice.

Toni, on the fringes of our little discussion, stares coldly at Brenda, who shrinks back and quickly adds, "Please," with a phony-sweet smile.

The response to Brenda's request is apathetic at best, and several residents seem to act as if they did not hear her. After all, she isn't someone they fear will report them to a superior. My eye catches a woman with tan skin beyond Brenda's counter, observing us, but clearly keeping her distance. I touch Charlotte's arm and nod my head at the woman.

"That's Lenore Flores," Charlotte whispers. "She's a resident. You haven't met her before."

Toni moves away and toward the large picture window across from the dining room. She opens her cell phone and punches in a number. Within a moment, Toni is alternating nodding and speaking.

She eventually closes with a series of nods.

Charlotte has missed none of it, and says to our group, "Let's move over to the library room and get out of Brenda's way." She raises her voice and adds, "Toni, why don't you come with us."

Romano, Toni, Freda, Charlotte, Meredith, and I saunter the short distance to the narrow, compressed room known as the library. We sit in the room's soft chairs, pulling them around until we nearly form a circle.

Interesting. I wonder what my clever sister has in mind now.

23

"I AM QUITE certain," Charlotte declares, "that Trudy's collapse was either from fatigue or a consequence of something she knows. If the latter, it would behoove us to uncover what that is."

What inside information my sister has, I don't know, but her caveat is like throwing down the gauntlet, at least in this little group, for someone to pick up, to see whatever might emerge from that act. I would not put it past Charlotte to propose a red herring to see if someone is threatened by it.

Freda's once-attractive face, lined and gouged from years of negativity, is contorted in what I have come to know as her typical frown. Her eyes, dark and obtrusive, scan each of us—though she says nothing.

To my surprise, Romano is the first to speak.

"I guess you're talking about Claire; that Trudy knows something about Claire and how she died."

"Exactly," Charlotte says, amiably, but if she's thinking what I'm thinking, she's wondering how Jerry Romano (aka Romeo, aka Santa Claus) is aware of mischief in Claire's demise. So far, aside from Freda's outing of the detective—and probably Toni as well—the investigation has been kept sub rosa, or at least we thought so. I do recall Charlotte saying how gossip spreads like wildfire in the Village.

"Well, supposing she does," Romano says, "how would that cause her to pass out?" He looks at each of us for some kind of cor-

roboration, hesitates, then adds, "Unless you're implying that someone wanted to keep her quiet and did something nasty to her."

It's hard for me to see Romano as venal, what with his North
Pole look and constant grin, but I guess bad guys can learn to put on
a convincing front. In fact, in this setting, at this time, flushed with
my glorious, and now…*girlfriend?*…Meredith, opening up to me a half
hour ago, I find it difficult to tune in to anything malicious. If there
were some sort of cloud hovering beneath me, I have no doubt I
would be floating on it.

Charlotte shrugs. "I have no idea. Just a random thought, a possibility we might want to keep in the backs of our minds."

Brusquely, Freda spits out, "If you ask me, Esther, that Jew lady,
poisoned Claire. I wouldn't be surprised if she did the same to Trudy!"
With her elbow, she nudges Toni, sitting beside her (uncomfortably,
I suspect, as I think she would rather be in the background, watching
and listening).

"Anything is possible," my cool sister says evenly.

"Or," Meredith says, and I can see that Freda is offensive to her,
"for all we know, even you could have done it."

"Look, girlie, I'm not a killer. Your grandmother was a different
kind of bird, but hard as it may be for you to get it, I really did like
her. She kept all her designs to herself, what she believed, how she
chose to live her life, her relationships and all, so it didn't bother me."

"Everything bothers you, Freda," I put in. "You have strong
opinions about every person and every attitude."

"Nothing wrong with that. The world is a hostile place. Got to
take the offensive. A little barb now and then helps keep the armor in
place."

"People need to get along," Romano says, with his customary
grin.

"I'm hoping," Charlotte changes the focus, "that we all come to
the merchant fair tomorrow morning. I would like to have a little private memorial for Claire in her apartment at about noon. You're all
invited, and I'll ask several others who knew Claire to join us. It will
be a quiet, caring tribute."

"Think I'll go stand in the hall," Toni says, as she rises. "Teacher
says I've been naughty." She laughs at her own attempt to be clever
and strolls away. As she leaves, Romano peruses her up and down,
and I am reminded of Charlotte's characterization of him as some sort
of Don Juan.

Before any more is said, Sam Capizi, Trudy's grandson, appears at the door to the library. Seeing us, he walks in and says, "The doctor thinks my grandmother might be able to recover. It could have been a stroke. She was wide awake and told me not to worry."

Those words are about the most Sam has ever strung together at one time, at least in my presence. He doesn't look particularly sad, but I imagine when a loved one has lived past ninety, their imminent demise is to be expected. It would be interesting to know how connected this lad had been with Trudy over the years. My sister, on the same page as me, asks just that.

"You and Trudy have been close...or not?" Charlotte asks.

"When I was little, she kept me for two years. Mother had...disappeared, and Father was off somewhere."

"By the way, Sam," Charlotte adds, "I understand you were originally going to rent the guest apartment here at Bigelow. What happened to that? Where are you staying?"

"Oh." Sam looks troubled, a show of confusion washes across his face and replies softly, "Grandma has a couch in her place. Been rooming with her."

Charlotte smiles her *I know more than you think* smile and stands.

"Well," she says, "I didn't really mean to call a meeting. Just thought we could all compare notes for a few minutes. Now that we know about Trudy's status, I'm sure there are things each of us has to do. By the way, Sam, tomorrow morning is our wonderful merchant's fair. If you need anything from the neighborhood vendors, be sure to stop by the auditorium."

Sam wheels about and strides away, a bit out of character for him, since when I have been around him, he has only strolled, not strode.

Freda rises and curls her lip, chin thrust upward, as she goes to the back of the library and to the newspaper rack. She pulls out a copy of the *New York Times* and plops down again in a soft chair, facing away from us.

As we all stand, Romano seems to want to stick with us. I look at Charlotte to see what she will say.

"Ah Romeo, Romeo, wherefore art thou...going? My little family and I have some private business to discuss."

"To be sure," he replies, again with a grin. "I'll check in with you later." He hesitates, as if an issue is still unsettled, and issues an addendum. "One of these evenings, Charlotte, I'd like to take you to

Anna's, the best little Italian café in Langhorne. What do you say?"

"To be discussed," Charlotte answers. She turns and, with Meredith and me following, leaves the library.

As we depart, I crane my neck and see Freda, head twisted around toward us, listening and watching.

I love it and so much appreciate Charlotte's skill in summarizing events. She does it effortlessly, as if it were the most natural and expected thing to do.

She has steered us to the little lounge area with the rattan furniture. After Meredith and I settle onto the floral pillowed chairs, Charlotte says, "That Sam boy is an anomaly. I once said he did not have the smarts or the energy to pull off a murder, and I still believe that. But something eerie is operating with him and I'd love to know what it is. Frankly, I don't think it concerns Claire, but I would not be surprised if it has a lot to do with Trudy. I learned from Doreen, the Village director, that Trudy has a healthy trust account. I wonder who the beneficiary could be.

"Freda, unappetizing as usual, may have gotten it right, though I did not appreciate the way she addressed you, Meredith. She is verbally critical, but I doubt she would be clandestinely vicious. With her, though, it is a good idea to be alert to whatever.

"Romano is an openly Pollyannaish character who thinks of himself as nature's gift to mature women. I know he savors me, but I have an aversion to toadying men. Could he have harmed Claire? I don't see any motive, but one can never be sure.

"And how about Esther? I believe Freda's ugly prejudice is merely a bias that leaves her wanting Esther to be the culprit. But, even with Esther's bent for religious evangelism, I have strong doubts about her propensity to do harm. It would violate her religious sanctions.

"So, of this little nest of people we just left, lots of maybes, but no certainties."

"Wow!" I say. "It's a pleasure to do business with you, Sis. I'm glad I'm on your side."

"All your *ifs*, *ands*, and *buts*, make sense," Meredith says, "leaving us with plenty of outsiders, or maybe other insiders, who are possibilities."

"Yes," Charlotte says. "That is why I want to hold the meeting in Claire's apartment once the fair begins. I want personally to consult with Wally about some things, and I would very much like to visit with Dr. Lyle Overstreet. His arrogant attitude about the elderly residents is an insult, an illumination of either carelessness or indifference, and I hope nothing worse."

"How could grandmother have triggered so many foul reactions? She was a dear person to me, and actually very soft-hearted."

"Which can put people off," Charlotte says. "As Freda said it, she kept her unusual parts out of the public eye, did not parade them around, and did not recruit others. Some folks view a quiet, closed-mouth person as a threat."

Meredith turns inward. Her loss intermittently rises to the surface and tugs at her heart. Tears come. With our new connection, I feel free to hold her close, and I do so.

24

NIGHT BRINGS murky corners and, though not nec-
essarily true, the sense that danger is only a shadow away. It is a cold,
windless evening, where any footsteps crunching upon the late fall
leaves would be heard at a distance. The three of us are in Charlotte's
apartment playing Bananagrams, a social spin-off of Scrabble. I am
amazed at Charlotte's ability to make words out of random letters.

A loud knock at our door causes us to jump.

"Who is it?" Charlotte calls out.

"Your friendly detective, Dick Tracy."

"Funny," Meredith says.

"So he thinks," I answer.

"Coming," Charlotte announces.

Hartunian shuffles in, hardly lifting his feet from the carpet. He
seems gleeful.

"The note you found in the victim's apartment, well, as it turns
out, the odd, block letters were snipped from a newspaper–but not
just any newspaper. They were snipped from the *New York Times*. My
people can tell by the font–Georgia–which is not your run-of-the-mill
typeface."

Meredith and I exchange glances; we both know who regularly
peruses the *New York Times*. I look at Charlotte to gauge her reaction.

"Oh my," she says, "over two-million people nationwide read
the *Times*."

"True, but there is a code for each location, and some are

printed at outposts to defray long-distance delivery costs. Here's where we zero in. The newsprint differs slightly at each locale. The perp's note is on paper printed in Bucks County, not far from where we stand."

"Yes, but detective," I say, "don't we already know that the offender is local? I mean the potential suspects are obviously from around here, so of course they would read the available *Times*."

"Well," Charlotte intrudes, "it is also possible that some folks subscribe directly from New York. They don't seem to mind that their paper arrives a day later."

Meredith says, as if speaking her thoughts aloud, "It would be a good idea to check the issues of the *Times* in the little library here, to see if any edition has sections cut out."

"Good thought," Charlotte says.

"My main reason for stopping in tonight," Hartunian says, as if our little exchange has been unimportant, "is to straighten out the details about tomorrow. Toni phoned me with the info about the old lady, Trudy. She said there was some suspicion about her taking ill. When all the vendors arrive in the morning, I would like to take every possible suspect aside and question her—or him—to see what contradictions might pop up."

"Wonderful, detective," Charlotte says. "But I mentioned to you that I thought we ought to hand pick a dozen or so of the most likely candidates and, at a specified time, invite them to a very personal little memorial gathering in Claire's apartment—the scene of the crime. A lot more is likely to, as you put it, *pop up* in those tight quarters than out in the big hall. I've already made plans for a little soft music to be playing, from tapes that had been sent to Claire by someone she was close to."

The look on Hartunian's face tells it all.

"Whoa. Okay. You're way ahead of me, little lady." He stops, thinking it over. "Yep, I agree. Let's do it," he says, as if granting permission—his official police way of retaining authority.

Charlotte smiles.

"If it's okay with you," she begins, as if asking for permission, "why don't we shoot for about noon. That way most, if not all, of the folks we want will be here."

Hartunian nods, seems suddenly to catch on to what we are doing, and asks, "What kind of game is that?"

"Bananagrams," I reply, not inviting him to join us.

"Oh," he says, but asks nothing else. "Think I'll go home and get a good night's sleep. Gonna drop into the twenties tonight."

"We'll look for you tomorrow, detective," Charlotte says. "Stay warm."

When he is gone, Meredith says, "Got him wrapped around your little finger, Charlotte."

"Not my intention. He is, however, easily maneuvered. I kind of like him. It's nice to be in cahoots with an honest official, which he seems to be."

"So, what do we do about the *New York Times*?" I ask.

"It's a fragile lead at best," Charlotte says. "I am certain that if Freda were cutting up a newspaper, she wouldn't leave the remnants around. Anyway, it's not her style."

"I suppose we ought to keep our eyes open to others who regularly get the paper," I suggest.

We resume our game, where each player takes twenty-one tiles and tries to use them all up by forming words. Charlotte wins when the last word she lays down is *adze*, which I learn is a wood-shaping, axe-like tool, but with an arched blade.

The evening wears on, and I take my leave of the two women. Meredith seems more fatigued by the day's hectic activities than Charlotte. I deeply want Meredith to join me in my apartment, spend the night with me, celebrate our newly acknowledged connection, but a sense of propriety, incongruously having to do with my older sister, cautions me to postpone.

Despite the cold, I meander through the exterior Village door and stand in the entry, absently studying the night. A half-moon shines directly above, providing enough light to outline, against the starry sky, silhouettes of the now blackened firs and pines.

With closed eyes, I breathe deeply and feel the sting as the below-freezing air enters my lungs. It is invigorating; a feeling rare in my California latitude. My deep breaths come again and again.

As the scrunch of footsteps sounds on dry leaves, I turn sharply to my left, and, despite my conviction that no one would be out to hurt *me*, feel an instantaneous flicker of fear.

Emerging from the trees is something white, then a figure surrounding it. Like a camera slowly coming into focus, the figure becomes good-old Jerry Romano, and the white, appearing strangely, internally illuminated, is, of course, his ample, Santa-like beard.

"Jerry, what in hell are you doing out there?"

Romano ambles up, flashing a snowy smile, pretends to punch me on the shoulder, and says, "It's a superb night for hiking, and this frigid temperature reminds me of home."

"Oh yes, Newfoundland. Brrrr. I can imagine how cold it gets there."

"This is nothing. I'm used to below-zero Celsius every day from November through March."

A thought hits me that perhaps some sleuthing can be applied here. "Uh, let me ask you a question, Jerry. If you don't mind telling me, do you subscribe to the *New York Times*?"

"Don't regularly subscribe. Do like to read it. I drive into Newtown every couple of days to purchase essentials. It's only a fifteen-minute trip each way. They have a newsstand that carries papers from all over. Even have an *LA Times*, in case you're interested."

"No thanks. When I'm away, I'm happy to have all those celebrity shenanigans out of my life."

"I'll bet you don't appreciate those dumb car chases on the TV every week, either."

"Inane. The media priorities are all twisted. Someone could win a Nobel Prize and it's ignored, but a bad dude who steals a car becomes the 'breaking news' lead story."

"Yeah, that's why I like the New York paper. It's for lofty intellectuals like me." He laughs raucously, pleased with his indulgent self-reference.

We move into the interior atrium, an area not heated but still twenty or more degrees warmer than the outside. Romano hardly seems to notice the difference, while I shiver visibly and try to warm my hands.

"Coming to the merchant fair tomorrow?" I ask.

"Sure. They have them off and on. This one is a little different, 'cause I know your sister requested this date."

He looks to the left and the right, as if checking to be sure no one is eavesdropping. In a confidential tone, presuming we are partners in some clandestine event, Romano whispers hoarsely, "Bet it has something to do with the sleuthing around she's been doing."

"Actually, it's to accommodate me," I hasten to say, ignoring his clandestine manner. "I have to return to my home in California in a few days, and she wanted me to check out all the interesting goodies from the neighboring communities. Who knows? I might find something appealing. Perhaps a homemade, local creation, that catches my fancy."

"Heard they're including the New Hope folks this time. Never did that before."

"I was in New Hope the other day with Charlotte and Meredith. Was introduced to a few folks, so it made sense for them to know about the fair."

"Okay with me," Romano says, waggling his head, as if he doesn't need to know my makeshift explanations.

"You know," he says, switching topics, "your sister is a pretty amazing female. I have a lot of experience with women and, I have to tell you, she's a crafty one–a lady who's smarter than most."

"I happen to agree with you," I reply. "I'm a plodder when it comes to intrigue, and she has the capacity to penetrate to the core of an issue. They say that Lincoln had that ability, maybe not a pure genius when it came to IQ, but able to brush away the cobwebs and see the essence of a problem."

"It's a gift," he says. "Wish I had it. I kind of float along, riding the crest of a wave, until, of course, somebody or something does me wrong. Then, I have to admit, I rise up like an avenging angel."

Hmm. Never have seen him in a rage about anything. Is he trying to alert me? Is he almost confessing? Is his chatter a ploy to deliberately diddle me? Truly a curious fellow, this Newfie character, one who bears watching, though I'm sure Charlotte would have a different take on him than I.

"Hope it isn't me you want to take revenge on."

"Hey, Charlotte's brother, you're an affable fellow, and I can't imagine you wanting to do me wrong."

"Neither can I. You're an...uh...*affable fellow* yourself."

"Nice that you think so. For me, it's more important if the little ladies around here think it."

Time for bed," I say. "Sleep well."

"Always do. While visions of sugar plums...well, you know."

His deliberate childlike put-on is too much for me, and I laugh. Romano laughs with me, but I wonder what hidden agenda may be lurking behind his laughter.

25

WITH THE MORNING comes noise. Since the guest apartment is close to the lobby area and the meeting rooms, I am awakened at 7:00 AM by a motor–two motors, actually–which later I learn are a buffer machine polishing the floor of the auditorium and a buzz saw to trim some of the outside trees with low-hanging branches. Even though the Village management lays out no money for the fair, they are vain enough to want everything to look clean and fresh.

I wonder if Charlotte and Meredith are awake, and am about to phone them when my room phone rings. The voice says, "Let's the three of us go to the dining room for an oatmeal and raisins breakfast. We can indulge in some of their vile coffee."

"Okay, Sis. I'll meet you in the dining room in seven minutes."

—

Soon we are seated in the sparsely populated large room. Charlotte, dressed in a cute blue and white blouse and vest, which make her look years younger, says, "After we eat, I'm going for a walk in the cold for a few minutes. Since there are several complicated strategies that still need to be sorted out, I would like some time alone with my thoughts."

"By yourself? Isn't that dangerous?" Meredith asks.

"I'm not sure. Could be, but I doubt it."

"Why do you like to put yourself at risk?" I ask.

"You know, one of my heroes was the naturalist, John Muir. Interesting fellow. Born in Scotland, grew up in Wisconsin raised by a tyrannical Presbyterian minister for a father who forced him to memorize the Bible. He had blazing blue eyes and a full, dark beard. His passion was to walk everywhere; sometimes fifty miles in a two-day period. He was religious, but differed from his father in that he believed God was evident not so much in man, but in nature."

"What has that to do with taking risks?"

"Patience. I'm getting to that. Muir was quoted as saying that his life goal was to 'learn the language of flood-storm and avalanche.' He once crawled to the very edge of the summit where Yosemite Falls cascaded down into the valley below, in order 'to feel what the water felt.' Others were terrified at the risks he took, but his quest was to become one with whatever he was trying to understand."

"Ah," Meredith says, "I get it."

"Hmm, okay. So you're onto something and need to clear away the cobwebs—and that takes unusual measures, including some risky actions like hiking into the woods by yourself," I add.

"You both got it. Now let's eat so I can be on my way."

I am tempted to tail her, not for any eavesdropping reasons, but for safety. As I watch Charlotte disappear into the grove of trees, my fear escalates, though the sensible part of me knows it is highly unlikely that a villain is hiding in the woods.

—

It is nine o'clock when Meredith and I see Charlotte emerge from the tall firs and pines and cedars, my almost seventy-year-old sister, her posture erect and elegant, lips in a firm, straight line, as if she is determined about something. When she reaches us at the Village entryway she allows that line to spread into a smile.

"Nothing like nature to clear one's head," she says.

Visibly relieved, Meredith replies, "You look like the cat that got the canary."

"Cats are stalkers. I do research. Sometimes I plumb internally to clarify what's buried in my elderly brain, and sometimes I consult with others to see what they let slip out."

"Are you going to tell us what you've come up with, or make us wait?" I ask.

"It's no good tossing out random possibilities. What I've done is come to some decisions about what and who need to be plumbed. It will all come out, as they say, in the wash."

She's not only clever, my sister, she's mysterious. What frosts me is that she seems to know how to proceed in all of this while I'm totally inert and about as creative as a hockey puck.

"I suggest we amble over to the auditorium and see how the set-up is coming. Most of the vendors should be here by now, laying out their wares."

"Do you have a list," I ask, "of the people you want to invite to Claire's apartment?"

"It's in my head. We'll see who shows up, but there are about thirteen or fourteen…uh…likely candidates I hope will be here."

"*Candidates*," Meredith says pensively, "quite a term for a killer!"

"If you like, we can call them suspects, though for them that is a more frightening label, and it obviously wouldn't fit for most."

"I like the word they use with amateur athletes, eager to turn pro," I put in. "They call them prospects, though jokingly some scouts have referred to the less-talented ones as suspects."

The three of us wind our way to the merchant fair, for what I anticipate will be the beginning of a most challenging yet interesting few hours. A bright sun, working hard to promote a comfortable November day, slices through the windows of the long, tunnel-like Village halls, brightening our path. I am hoping it is an omen, and a light will shine on our investigative path as well.

The first thing Charlotte does in the basement room is approach Wally Burt, who is wearing a bright, crimson sweater. He hovers over his table, which is decorated with an eye-catching green and white paisley tablecloth, adorned with two-dozen large platters of food covered with plastic wrap.

He and Charlotte wander over to the left front corner of the large room, now bustling with others similarly arranging their products, and stand together. They quietly converse near an outlandishly large American flag that rises from a tube-stand planted in a round ceramic tub.

Seven or eight minutes pass as they stand near the flag, talking without much movement, making it hard to determine the emotional level of their conversation. I have the incongruous thought that they would make an elegant patriotic picture: the white-haired matriarch with her blue-and-white outfit and the tall, gaunt gentleman, dressed in red.

When Wally returns to his display table, Charlotte peers about, paying particular attention, it seems, to the entryway, where residents are just beginning to arrive. She then sees something that moves her. She strides, in her purposeful way, toward the far wall, near the door, smiling at a lone figure standing immediately, unobtrusively, inside. It is the woman she mentioned to me just yesterday, the tan-skinned and, at least to me, obscure, Lenore Flores.

Curious. I watch avidly while they talk for several minutes, as with Wally, neither is particularly animated.

I turn my attention to the vendors, and see table after table of appealing colors and shapes, along with their invisible odors and fragrances. Another food vendor is now set up besides Wally's, aromas waft about in the tranquil air within the auditorium. It's been said that the elderly are inflexible about their fragrance habits—the common stereotype is that they mostly wear lavender. As such, it's a bit surprising to me to see at least two perfume-cologne stations, their signs and oversized posters advertising the latest in fashionable scents.

There are several garment tables, including the one across from Wally, with a fold-up sign that reads "Go Fur It," attended to by both Delbert and Evangeline Kraus.

One elderly woman has commandeered a table for her needle-point creations of afghans and pillow covers, while a younger woman, looking chic in a wide-brimmed, aqua-blue hat, displays colorful comforters, from twin to queen-sized, which, I would imagine, she has fabricated herself.

To my surprise, I spot a table monitored by a tall woman bending over a sign that reads "Vision Aid." I recognize her as Helen Cumberland, her low-cut blouse, and silver cross, visible even from a distance. Business is business. Of course, she's here.

Near the right periphery of the crowd of tables is one that strikes my fancy: chocolates and homemade fudge, a must-visit locale for me.

Meredith points and lets out a little gleeful giggle. "Ooh, look at that!" A man and a woman unknown to me are monitoring a table containing a hand-printed sign that reads, "Electronics, Cell Phones, Blackberries, i-Pods, Computers; See and Hear Your Grandchildren."

"Clever pitch," Meredith says.

Another surprise for me is that Tommy Cox, the exercise maven, has wandered in and is casually meandering from table to table. I am again impressed with his physique—trim and powerful. With his pen-

chant for endorsing bodily health, my guess is he will avoid the chocolate display and perhaps gravitate toward a table, against the wall and
close to an electrical outlet, promoting yogurt shakes.

I search for Romeo, but do not find him, at least not yet. Some
thirty residents are now in the auditorium, a few, as I know to expect,
in wheelchairs and a couple with walkers. Pushing a wheelchair
through the entryway is Dr. Frederick Doolittle and, at his side, Dr.
Lyle Overstreet. Both of them cannot be on duty at the same time, so
one made a special trip for the fair.

Charlotte has serious suspicions about Overstreet. She told me
that he had enrolled in medical school planning to become a psychia-
trist. An attempt, she believed, to explain his own messed-up childhood. He switched to general medicine when the depth of the psychological studies got too close to his pain. How she knew this, I'm
not quite sure, but I would guess it might have come from Doolittle.
I'm glad both men showed up. I presume another physician is holding
down the fort in the medical center. It seems perfect that it is Doolittle assisting a physically challenged patient rather than Overstreet.

Freda enters, squinting through half-closed eyes at the whole gala
spread. For the first time, I wonder if she has vision problems. She
moves slowly about, inspecting the exhibits, her face glowering in
what I read as a harsh critique.

Charlotte, returns from her talk with Lenore Flores. She spies
Freda and says to Meredith and me, "Excuse me for a minute," then
crosses over and touches Freda's arm.

Freda recoils, but then seems to relax when she sees that it's
Charlotte. They stand together for several minutes, as more residents
move into the bustling room. Charlotte leaning in, talking; Freda
drawn back, listening. Charlotte, at least in the beginning, seems to do
most of the talking, but, after a time, Freda leans in, her look changing
from curiosity to defiance. Though perhaps that is my bias.

The two remain in that configuration for a long while—Charlotte
with her usual nonthreatening manner, Freda with her familiar, aggressive style. My teacher's need to change people and my humanistic
need to make nice causes me to ponder why Freda can't be more amiable.

When my sister returns to our corner vantage point at what
might be seen as the apex of an isosceles triangle, she looks flushed
and self-satisfied.

"You've been a busy little bee," I say. "I hope your interviews have paid off."

"It's like a giant crossword puzzle with too many pieces," Charlotte says. "Yet, I see streaks of light pouring into the dark corners, illuminating some possible fits and connections. I do believe the meeting in Claire's apartment will pay dividends."

Meredith smiles at her—that beautiful smile of affection—and says, "You are something else. I love your optimism. I wish that Hartunian character had half your insight."

"Well, he wears a badge and works within the system. That puts a clamp on things. I have the luxury of not being a cop, not raising hackles. People are a lot more likely to talk to me."

Toni, our undercover cop, enters the auditorium. At her side, perhaps curiously, but maybe not, is Jerry Romano.

26

BY ELEVEN THIRTY, there are maybe seventy-five residents milling about, perhaps a quarter of whom reside in Bigelow Village.

"Not a bad turnout," I mention to Charlotte.

"One-hundred would have been better. Of course the total number is not significant in our hunt for Claire's killer. What is critical is that the key figures, suspects, prospects, or whatever we call them, are present and can be coaxed into Claire's apartment."

I nod in agreement.

"Brenda isn't here," Charlotte says, "but that doesn't bother me. She is hardly culpable in all this. I was hoping that Oscar would come, not so much because he's a possible culprit, but because he could prove valuable in confirming the prescriptions he had dispensed."

"What about the young grandson of Trudy's, Sam Capizi?" Meredith asks. "To me, he's an odd character who hasn't explained himself very well."

"When Augustus arrives, I want to put him onto taciturn little Sammy's trail. I think he may be trying to—as gang members say it—*off* his grandmother so he can collect on the inheritance. I think the doctors here ought to do a toxic screen on Trudy, just as they did on Claire, to see if she's been overdosed with something."

"Good idea," I chip in. "Sammy's an enigma to me. If he was honest about that assigned business in New York, how come he's been hanging out around here all this time?"

A dark-bearded fellow with curly hair and pale blue eyes is per-forming music near the American flag. He is talented and looks soul-ful. Dexterous fingers move gracefully along the neck of a well-worn acoustic guitar. His set list includes classical pieces by Francisco Tarrega and Joaquin Rodrigo, and folk melodies by Bob Dylan, Joan Baez, Pete Seeger and Arlo Guthrie.

I look at Charlotte, who says, "You won't believe it, but Romano is paying that guy two-hundred dollars to play for a couple of hours."

"Romano? Romeo?"

"Not too many people know this, but our bearded friend is roll-ing in money. Likes the company and ambience here, but actually could afford much more luxurious digs if he wanted."

"He is a damned curious character," Meredith says, "but this place is full of them."

"Men and women alike," I add.

"Tell you what," Charlotte changes the subject. "It's time to de-liver the invitations to the 'memorial' in Claire's apartment. I suggest the three of us divide the chore in the most logical way possible. Mer-edith, why don't you approach the doctors first; someone will take over for the patient Doolittle wheeled in, and he will be happy to come. With Overstreet, who is a sucker for beautiful women, you'd be the best person to invite him. You might expect resistance, but I'm pretty sure he will agree to join us out of guilt and curiosity.

"Greg, I spoke with Wally, but mostly to ask him some other questions and request that he bring a few of his to-die-for pastries to Claire's apartment. It would be good for you to take Wally, and you'll be able to see if someone will monitor his table for an hour or so. Wait a minute, I forgot. I haven't seen her yet, but Wally told me his daughter, Jessica, would be here, so she can handle his goods. While you're there, also invite the other New Hope folks at the next table over—the Kraus couple—since they knew Claire.

"Esther has arrived with her husband, so I'll take her. I know she was critical of Claire's nonreligious bent, but you can bet she'll feel flattered to be included in the inner circle of folks who get asked to this little private celebration. I already invited the rather shadowy Le-nore Flores. You don't know her, but I consider Lenore someone an investigator would refer to as *a person of interest*. A few times in the last couple of months, though she acted shy and tentative, I saw her show some inquisitiveness about Claire. She was taken by surprise when I asked her, but thanked me and said okay.

"I'll also ask Romano, since he has an ongoing sort of 'thing' for me. Well, he has a thing for *all* women. I'm certain he'll respond enthusiastically to my personal invitation.

"Meredith, when you finish with the doctors, how about seeing if Tommy, our muscular P.E. instructor, would be willing to come along. As it relates to Claire's death, he's a long shot when in terms of motive, but he's been popping up in different places lately. His curiosity will get the best of him, especially if a trim physical specimen, such as you, invites him.

"And Greg, how about you asking Helen Cumberland, our ultra-tall, ultra-religious Vision-Aide lady, to join us. Much as she had her issues with Claire, we know she has been in the apartment, and will certainly be anxious to see what the celebration is all about.

"As to Freda, pardon my colorful language, but she's a kick in the ass! I told her about the little gathering and, with her suspicious bent—paired with her shrewdness—she said, 'Ah, clever, Charlotte, clever; get all the possibles in one room. I wouldn't miss it!'

"Have I left anyone out?"

To me, this whole scene is beginning to play out like a movie, all the characters assembled while the detective reviews each person's motives. Perhaps a bit grandiose to think of my big sister in the same vein as a movie detective, but, with her recent interviews, discoveries, and insights into the mystery, why the hell not?

Meredith asks, "What time shall we tell them? It's 11:40."

"12:15 will work," Charlotte answers. "I have the key to the apartment, and I'll go over there just at noon for some last-minute preparations."

Augustus Hartunian walks into the now-crowded room, sees us, and hurries over, but not before waving to his aide, Toni, to join him.

"Okay," he says officiously, "let's get this little show on the road."

When Charlotte smiles at him and wiggles her finger back and forth, as if in a mock scold, he retreats, and says, "Uh, so what's the plan?"

"Oh, detective, I hope it's okay with you that we are about to invite the most promising prospects into Claire's apartment for our little private memorial. We so much appreciate your expertise in these matters, and you and Toni being in the room will be the key element in legitimizing what we'll try to do."

I'm not sure he quite gets the crux of Charlotte's words of obei-sance. Meredith and I exchange amused smiles. After all, in the grand climaxes of mysteries like this, the cops are present but the crimes are almost always solved by the astute nonprofessional. There is a feeling of suspense in the air, and, in this moment, I feel indescribably proud of my intrepid sister.

"Could I speak with you alone, Ms. Charlotte?" Hartunian asks in a subdued tone. "Got some more evidence to show you from the forensics lab, but I'm afraid it's a mystery."

"By all means," Charlotte says, and moves to a corner with the detective. She listens attentively for a few minutes. Charlotte smiling knowingly and then shakes Hartunian's hand.

She returns in a moment, and says, "I clued him into the timeframe and alerted him to the invitations to be extended."

That is all she gives us. She keeps whatever had confounded the detective to herself, so that Meredith and I head off to our assign-ments in the dark. I'm hoping every invitee says yes, but how they respond and exactly what they say, I can only report from the those I personally ask.

As I approach Wally's table I notice that Jessica, his young daughter, has arrived. They are pointing at items on their colorful ta-blecloth and gabbing away, so I feel a bit awkward interrupting. But Wally sees me and extends a hand.

"Ah, hello there, Charlotte's brother. Very good to see you. A most successful event, don't you think? First one of these I've at-tended. I believe it's the first time the New Hope folks have been invited."

"That's my sister's doing. She thought your wonderful products needed to be available here at the Village."

"I agree. You remember Jessica, my lovely daughter."

"Sure. Great server. How you doing, Jess?"

She smiles, a cute teen-age smile with perfect teeth, and busies herself with chores. The silly and certainly self-centered thought strikes me that, twenty years ago, she might have looked at me with interest. But today I'm an old guy, her dad's acquaintance. And what am I thinking anyway? I seem to have successfully wooed Meredith, my Meredith. I look over my shoulder to see her walking across the room, and I turn back to Wally.

"Well, I just wanted to be sure you knew the time for the little gathering at Claire's apartment. It's 12:15. You know how to get there."

Wally nods innocently. "I packed up a box full of my desserts. Charlotte also asked if I'd bring a couple of bottles of wine. California reds, by the way."

"Great! We'll pay you for your contributions. Good that Jessica is here to watch over your table."

I turn and move the few yards to where the other New Hope folks are set up. Delbert Kraus and his wife are adjusting five or six, mannequins, each three-feet in height, that appear to be molded from mottled glass adorned with elegant designer clothes. Delbert turns from them and greets me with a grin and a slap on my back. His wife, Evangeline, offers a pained smile but says nothing.

"Wow," I say to him, "Those mannequins are unique. Never seen any like them."

"That's because we mold them ourselves. They make our shop special."

"I'm sure that's true. They really catch the eye."

"Thanks! And I need to thank your sister for inviting us."

"Charlotte has planned a small, private memorial for a few friends of Claire's in Claire's apartment in about half an hour. She asked me to invite you. Do you have someone to watch your merchandise?"

Delbert looks confused, but seems to catch on quickly. "Freddy, our helper, is right outside. We could ask him. Uh, how many folks will be there?"

"I don't know, maybe fifteen or so. People who knew Claire. So, can we count on you?"

"We didn't know her very well, but..."

"No, I want to go." Evangeline says assertively. "It is the respectful thing to do."

"Of course, dear. I'm happy to honor the lovely lady."

Evangeline is an odd duck. A pretty woman, I guess between fifty-five and sixty years old. I wonder what great tragedy occurred in her life that twisted her into such sadness. Delbert looks to be in his early sixties. I also wonder if they have any children.

"How long will the gathering last?" Delbert asks.

"Not sure, but certainly not more than an hour, maybe less."

"I'll go out to the van and ask Freddy if he'll sit in here and watch for us," he says to his wife. Then he turns to me and says, "Freddy doesn't work in our shop, but he is a nice young fellow who helps us sometimes." He pauses, and, with a nod toward the outside wall, adds, "Likes to read comic books."

"Great," I say. "I have a few more people to invite. Do you know which is Claire's apartment? It's in the more intensive care wing."

"Uh, well, we'll ask Wally. Maybe we can walk down there with him."

As I move away, I realize that Delbert seemed stuck for the barest instant when I asked if he knew where the apartment was. Damn, there are a lot of folks who *could* have been visitors to Claire's place.

Next stop, Helen Cumberland. She is seated at her table, bent over what looks like an old-fashioned electric Facit typewriter, though it is not attached to a power source. As I move closer, I can see that it is producing braille labels, and that Helen is copying them in to the machine from a list of prescriptions. Displayed on her countertop next to the machine is a series of vision-type offerings, including ads for glasses by Prada, as well as bifocals and contact lenses, all worn by gorgeous models. A couple of large posters of handsome men and women, all white and with impossibly piercing eyes–mostly blue and green–are mounted around the long table, to illustrate the desirability of these products to the beautiful people of the world.

"Hello, Ms. Cumberland. Glad to see you here."

"Yes, well, our merchandise is widely used at Bigelow. It makes sense to promote it in person."

Before I can respond, two elderly women I don't recognize stop beside me. One says to Helen Cumberland, "You saved my life, dear, with those new glasses. They brighten up my days." The other adds, "Me, too. Those braille labels make all the difference with my meds."

Ms. Cumberland smiles. "Glad to be of service."

The women move on, and I say, "Speaking of service, we are about to hold a small memorial honoring Claire Hazelton. It will be in her apartment at 12:15. Her granddaughter asked if we'd go around and invite those who knew her."

"Well, I knew her, but I can't say she was my friend."

"We're aware of that, but you did provide some needed assistance to her, and you came to her apartment to help out."

There is a silence, so I add, "Charlotte also asked that you come. It will be simple and reasonably brief." Cumberland still hesitates, so I ask, "Do you have someone to watch your table for a few minutes?"

At last she says, "Well, sir..."

I am taken aback by the response and use of "sir" and catch the slightest hint of contempt, a deliberate sarcasm, in its use. Though perhaps she is trying to show me some semblance of respect.

"As to that…there is nothing here to steal, except maybe this old braille writer. But it's pretty unwieldy and would be next-to-impossible for a frail, older person to carry off."

I smile. She isn't the only one who has disdain for the very folks they curry as customers.

"Wonderful, Helen," I say, hoping my use of her first name will make her feel more welcome. "We'll look for you in a little less than half an hour."

When I leave her location, I gaze about, searching for Charlotte, and at last see her, still gabbing away with Romano. I can only presume she has already spoken with Esther.

Across the room is Tommy, the coach, supporting his strapping body with a hand against the wall, legs crossed at the ankles, looking smug, no doubt feeling complimented by the beautiful female next to him. I can tell, even from a distance, that Meredith, winsome and smiling, is working on him. Based on the nodding and smiling he returns, there appears to be no question that Tommy will be joining us in Claire's apartment.

Meredith's other assignment was to approach the two doctors, and, though I don't see them, I have no doubt she has tendered the invitation and that they will come. A full house, I think. This will be quite a production.

27

THE TALL AND lean Oscar Ott shows up before 12:15. Charlotte has left for the apartment, so I approach him and explain our plan.

"Delighted. This…uh…exhibit is impressive. Haven't been to one before. Charlotte asked me, and I wasn't sure, but she is a convincing lady."

"She is. And this little spin-off is to properly honor Claire."

"Ah, yes. The woman of the mysterious demise. I would love to know what really happened to her."

"So would I. Maybe we'll know more after the memorial gathering. The meeting is in apartment number 106, in the intensive care wing."

I smile as I remember that Charlotte called referred to Ott as Double O. Ott seems like a pleasant fellow, critical to the health of so many here at the Village. Prescriptions rule the roost in a retirement complex, since almost every resident is under some type of medical regimen. It was Ott who first mentioned the possibility of a selenium overdose.

Meredith walks up, looking bemused.

"What a jerk."

"Who?"

"The bodybuilder. Thinks he's heaven's gift to women. Every sentence is a cliché or some hackneyed axiom. He isn't mean or anything, just clearly narcissistic and boring."

"I recall he thought Claire was kind of dumb for not buying into his exercise agenda."

"When I invited him, he said something like, 'Oh the blind lady with the staring blue eyes who didn't believe in exercise.' I'm afraid he'll be little more than a distraction."

"Well, Charlotte thought it a good idea for him to attend. Maybe we'll find out why."

"Is everyone accounted for?" Meredith asks. "I mean, are all the key participants committed to attending?"

"Far as I know."

Spending so much time with Meredith like this following our...breakthrough...is frustrating. We have business to conduct, a meeting to run, perhaps a crime to solve. I'd much rather disappear with her into my rented rooms and celebrate. It seems odd and somewhat awkward to propose anything personal when this massive climax is about to occur. Contrary to the mindsets of twenty-year olds, those of us in our fifties are anything but passionless, impotent, or indifferent. I yearn for closeness, for unfettered romance, and for the pleasurable feeling of body next to body doing...whatever.

I lean over, hoping not to trespass, and kiss Meredith on her neck.

"Nasty man," she says. "Don't start something you can't finish."

I want to describe in detail what Charlotte has done in Claire's apartment, because I believe it will make for a clearer picture of what I presume will transpire.

She doesn't create some sort of New Age inner sanctum, with burning incense and atmospheric far-east background music. My clever sister has arranged a low-light ceremony. Yes, there are candles, at least five, on the mantel over the fireplace. The music is modern, from one of the tapes she found in Claire's rooms, presumably from her lover; Sinatra performing, "I've Got You Under My Skin."

Along with the couch, two armchairs, and the four hardback kitchen chairs, Charlotte has managed to procure a half-dozen others that fold. The chairs are arranged in a semi-circle so that the seating resembles a curved moon facing the fireplace.

To all purposes, everything is set for a memorial ceremony, with no hint of confrontation about the cause of Claire's death. Great touch about Frankie-boy's song, since she can observe the reaction on people's faces as they enter and settle into their places.

In her intuitive way, Charlotte seems to know that loss and lone-liness can make a person ill or dreadfully despondent—and certainly could cause an open display of emotion: so much for the unmasking of Claire's secret lover—if she indeed will be in the room.

As to the murderer, we have yet to see what my amateur sleuth sister is planning that might be able to create a breakthrough with either a confession or an irrefutable accusation.

The time has come. Meredith and I enter Claire's apartment at exactly 12:16 PM. Along with Charlotte, the only others in the room are Freda, seated on the sofa, her arms crossed, and Jerry Romano, standing near Charlotte by the kitchen table, his Santa-beard's white-ness an eye catcher in the muted light.

Charlotte gives us a knowing smile and busies herself with the pastries and wine goblets arranged on the pass-through counter to the kitchen.

In a moment, Detective Hartunian and Toni enter. Charlotte motions for them to step into the kitchen, where she speaks confi-dentially, to request, I imagine, that they make themselves unobtru-sive. Freda, of course, scowls at the sight of them and nods her head slowly.

Wally enters through the propped-open door, followed by his entrepreneur neighbors from New Hope. He gazes about the room and smiles, as if approving. Del and Evangeline Kraus sit on the couch next to Freda, Evangeline with her usual dour countenance, her hand gripping her husband's arm. Though it is hard to see in the subdued light, her face looks blotchy, as if she had been crying, which doesn't surprise me, as she seems to be living with some eerie histor-ical angst.

Wally approaches Charlotte and they talk softly as he helps her, with his epicurean expertise, to arrange the snacks in an appealing configuration—which is beyond my understanding, since finger food is just finger food.

One after another, Esther and her husband, coach Tommy Cox, (looking out of place and quizzical), Helen Cumberland, and the two doctors (seeming disgruntled, at least as far as Overstreet is con-cerned), walk into the room.

"Find a place to sit, folks," Charlotte says. "We'll begin the pro-gram shortly."

Lenore Flores, tentative as a frightened kitty, sort of sneaks in from the hall and slides along the wall until she reaches a back-row folding chair. She sits with her legs to the side and looks out at the assembly. I wonder what she must have experienced in her life prior to Bigelow Village to make her so timid. Freda seems to react in an odd, spirited way that's difficult to pinpoint upon seeing Lenore enter.

Of those I know about, only Oscar Ott is yet to arrive.

"When our tribute is over," Charlotte says, "we invite you to toast Claire with a glass of wine and some wonderful pastries, brought to us by Wally Burt, a good friend and proprietor of the splendid New Hope eating establishment known as Nutrition for The Heart-y."

As she finishes the announcement, the pharmacist, Double O, walks in, nodding his head in apology for being tardy.

It is now a full house, with most attendees seated. Charlotte, the police officers, and I stand. Meredith is seated in a back-row chair in front of me, my hands rest upon her shoulders. Delicious!

"First off," Charlotte begins, "I would like us to hear from Claire's lovely granddaughter, Meredith Hazelton, who, some of you may know, lost not only her grandmother but her best friend. Please, Meredith, the floor is all yours." Charlotte steps over and pushes the button to stifle the music, catching Sinatra's voice after he sings, "…deep in the heart of me."

I'm surprised that Meredith has been asked to speak, but she is obviously prepared. She and Charlotte must have discussed this and planned it in advance.

Meredith rises and moves to the front of the group, the fireplace and five glowing candles at her back. I also notice that Charlotte has positioned herself so that she can monitor all those present. I look around at the attendees, aware of the intense expressions on the faces of the mousey Lenore Flores, the sullen Freda Graham, and, of course, the ever-sad Evangeline Kraus. Tommy Cox is sitting on one of the kitchen hardback chairs, extending and flexing both arms in a personal and quiet form of exercise. The rest of those in the room show little or no emotion, their looks relatively impassive, but none-theless attentive.

"I doubt," Meredith begins, "if any of you know that my grand-mother Claire was my Rock of Gibraltar, my listening post, as em-pathic as the most skilled therapist, caring to a fault and utterly self-less. She would rather die than ever hurt another. In fact, I would not be surprised if that is what happened." She stops, as a collective hush descends on the room.

Rather die? What is Meredith referring to?

She resumes, "But more of that in a moment. Historically, Claire was a Californian for years, and, in her youth, believe it or not, was a decorated police officer."

Meredith looks at Hartunian, but the officer seems lost in his own ruminations and shows nothing. My sense of this nice-enough detective is that he often shows nothing. Not dense, but certainly distracted.

"Her blindness made her dependent on others, yet she still was ferociously independent, gratefully relying on the kindness of friends for transportation and guidance when in unfamiliar places—but for almost nothing else.

"Despite some horrific life events, Claire was an optimistic person who felt the roses on the bush, not the thorns. Again, for those who did not know her well, let me say that she was a profound lover, and when she loved, she loved with all her heart. I was the fortunate recipient of that love.

"But so were others. She marched to the beat of her own drum, and loved whom she pleased and how she pleased. One of those loves was a tender partnership for many years in California, which, unfortunately, seemed to dissolve when her blindness developed."

Someone within the room responds with a little gasp. Esther Hahn looks harsh and foreboding. Freda seems to be growing more agitated. Charlotte misses none of it.

"There is some recent evidence that my dear grandmother was deeply connected to someone in the general Bigelow Village neighborhood. She was, however, a private person, and kept that relationship to herself."

In stunned silence, I listen to this woman I am now delighted to think of as my *girlfriend*. As Charlotte has for the past few days, Meredith seems to be cleverly building toward a climax confrontation about Claire's mysterious death. The true purpose of this memorial gathering is progressively going to slide into focus, and Meredith is orchestrating it with remarkable aplomb, despite the heartache she must be feeling.

"Her death took some of us by surprise, since she seemed relatively healthy, showing little if any symptoms of illness. One cannot say, as is so often the...misguided and insulting diagnosis with the elderly, that Claire Hazelton died of old age."

As she says these words, Meredith looks calmly, but intensely, at

Dr. Lyle Overstreet, who tilts his head slightly and frowns. In my imagination, he would love to get into Meredith's pants, and here she is impugning his indifferent views about the Bigelow residents.

"One also cannot say that she was a careless person and, because of her blindness, made errors that contaminated her body and caused it to rebel against her. My wonderful grandmother was meticulous and thorough. Most importantly, she savored her life, even with the obvious boundaries her disability created."

Charlotte takes several steps to the right, so that she is looking more directly into the half-circle of faces. Her eyes are narrower than usual, and she seems immersed in deep thoughts. Some sixth sense—which she seems to possess in abundance—tells her I am staring at her. She lifts her eyes for a bare instant and smiles at me, though her smile is inscrutable.

Meredith, too, sees Charlotte move and I catch a wry smile on her lips as she continues.

"So here we are, celebrating a life, not a death. All of you here are the ones who, as far as we can tell, had a connection with Claire. Some deeper, others more casual. I want to conclude my remarks and turn the meeting back to Charlotte, one of Claire's closest friends. First, let me say that my grandmother was a precious person, and I shall miss her in my heart-of-hearts until the day a memorial is held for me. I cannot imagine anyone wanting to do her harm. I cannot imagine it, but, ladies and gentlemen, though it is a terrible thing to realize, I am sad to report to you, that is precisely what happened."

The crowd buzzes, heads turn, a few of the folks appear startled by her closing words. Meredith returns slowly to her chair, green eyes glassy with tears.

As if to savor the moment of confusion, Charlotte waits for several seconds, then moves deliberately to the front of the group. She stands erect, with what might be described as an imperious look. The candles flicker behind her, seeming otherworldly and deliciously supernatural—as if she belongs on the SyFy channel—with a glimmering halo above her head.

I notice the two police officers standing at the edge of the kitchen, Toni nodding and grinning, Hartunian, ankles and arms crossed, partially bemused. I can tell he is used to running the show and doing so a hell of a lot differently.

"My friends," Charlotte begins, "before I go into a rather probing bit of analysis about lovely Claire Hazelton's unusual death, I would love it if any of you would care to say a few words to honor her memory."

The room is silent. I try to gauge the mood, and it seems that fear is present, unusual for a memorial service—unless people are imagining their own demise—but also a kind of reverence, which might be expected.

At last, not to my surprise, Freda stands.

"Claire was an iconoclast, like me, only nicer. I tend to give the finger to the world. But she would more likely shrug and say, instead, that we have to understand how sad the trespassers are; give them a little space; not judge them. There are a lot of folks who resented Claire's position on things. I guess that's their right, but it's not their right to hurt her for them."

She sits abruptly. Charlotte seems to absorb Freda's declaration with her usual tolerance, displaying no emotion one way or the other. My own thought is that Freda could well be the master deflector in the group.

After a moment, Wally rises, steps forward, and turns to face his companions.

"Good people, for most of my adult years I have been a food person—baking, cooking, and serving, as best I could, new tastes and unique flavors. One morning, Charlotte Smart, everybody's friend," Wally says, pausing to nod at Charlotte, "…brought to my humble New Hope establishment her good friend, Claire Hazelton. Oh, I can't tell you what a beautiful connection was established from that day on!

"We were like two reunited old buddies. Compatriots on our life journeys; her droll humor was a tonic for my hectic schedule. Whenever the two of them came for a morning breakfast, I could count on my day being enriched, glowing, a silent chuckle just below the surface.

"Like the song, with amazing grace, Claire was blind and yet could see. I have only one good eye, but, I am sure you will understand my message when I say, my dear friend, Claire, had two.

"I can't tell you what clear perceptions this amazing woman had. Her death diminishes me. To paraphrase the poet, John Donne, she was involved in mankind, and did not send to know for whom the bell tolls; it tolled for her."

For an instant, he cannot go on. A sob escapes Wally as he looks down and to the side, then out over the group.

He closes with a brief, final comment. "I miss her."

A new respect for Wally Burt—that he would be so emotionally open in front of the whole group—spreads through me like a cozy warmth. Around the room, several folks dab at their eyes, obliterating any chance to focus on anyone who might be unduly smitten by Wally's words.

Oddly, at least as I see it, Jerry Romano steps forward.

"Yes," he begins as if what he is about to say will be an addendum, "Claire could see, and, alas, I'm afraid she saw through me. I'm not so terrible, but my foibles are known to most of you. Not even her granddaughter knows this, but, one day, maybe six months ago, Claire sat across the table from me in the dining room, and, after we finished eating, she smiled her wise smile and said, '*O Romeo, Romeo! Wherefore art thou Romeo?*'

"When I asked her what comes next, she said, 'You, my friend, don't know who the hell you are. You keep running around looking for yourself. The women are camouflage. You're really trying to find Jerry Romano.' I resented her for a few weeks, but, finally, in one of my introspective and private moments, acknowledged she was correct."

A ripple of laughter goes through the room, chasing away, for the moment, the somber tone.

Romano also finds it amusing, looking about the room, seeming to be soaking up the attention, and cracks a smile, stretching his white beard to show his pink lips and almost-as-white teeth.

"Truth comes in a lot of different packages," he says in closing. "Though I can't say I am a completely changed man, I discovered a powerful truth for me through this remarkable woman."

With several folks praising Claire, I wonder if the list of suspects will dwindle down to those who say nothing. Charlotte, of course, will not be taken in by hyperbole, even if I seem to be.

Dr. Frederick Doolittle stands, does not move to the front, but softly begins to speak.

"Ms. Hazelton was not my patient, though I did see her a few times over the years. I appreciated her candid style. Uh…Dr. Segal is the third member of our Bigelow medical staff, and, since he was not invited to the merchant's fair, he agreed to be on duty so we—Dr. Overstreet and I—could attend both that function and this…uh…memorial gathering. Dr. Overstreet had been Ms. Hazelton's primary care physician, and knew her much better than I. But…uh…we are all terribly distraught by her death, since, as you all surely know, the primary function of the medical profession is to prolong life."

He seems confused for an instant, then smiles at the assembly. "That's all I have to say."

A hush seems to fall over the group, the mood restless and expectant. Discomfort stretches across several faces. What is about to come may be confrontational, a scary prospect for at least a few in attendance.

Charlotte moseys over to the front and takes a moment to peruse the faces of those looking up at her. With a conciliatory smile at the audience (after all, the subject-matter is obviously not all eulogy), she turns toward the kitchen area and gestures to Meredith and Toni. The two women walk forward, carrying trays of wine glasses to the seated guests. Clever, I think, since the thrust is likely to change; it is a grand idea to have a little refreshment break.

A few eschew the grape, but several reach for a goblet, as my sister lifts hers and says, "A toast to Claire Hazelton. May thoughts of her give us all pleasure for many years to come."

The wine is sipped and Charlotte is about to speak again when suddenly someone dashes into the room, stopping abruptly by the number of people.

In the startled silence, young Sam Capizi blurts out, "She's dead. Trudy is dead!"

28

TO SAY THAT the news shatters the ambience in Claire's apartment would be an understatement. The two doctors stand at once, and Overstreet almost shouts at Sam.

"How do you know? Did Dr. Segal tell you?"

"I was outside her recovery room, and could hear the beeping turn to a long drone. A nurse and the doctor ran in, but came out a few minutes later."

"I'll go," Doolittle says. "No need for both of us."

I look at Charlotte and Detective Hartunian, both of whom seem on high alert. Charlotte nods to the detective and he, along with Sam and Dr. Doolittle, hurries out of the room.

Charlotte turns back to the assembly, looking somewhat shaken, since this new development could easily upstage what she is attempting. The room is alive with low voices, both residents and service providers seeming to struggle to absorb the information. Death of any kind is sobering, and Bigelow is a relatively close-knit community. I wonder how my sister will handle this interruption.

"Good people," she says, "we have an important agenda here in this room, which ought not to be postponed. I'm sure we will get a more complete report about Trudy when Dr. Doolittle returns. For the moment, I propose that we take a couple of minutes to sit in silence to honor Trudy, each in our own way."

Sharp woman, my Charlotte. The room is still, except for Esther Hahn's husband, Elmore, who is humming softly to himself. She does not try to stop him. In this quiet time, I ponder what the true culprit must be feeling. I wonder if there is a sense of something closing in.

After more than a minute of silence Charlotte says, "Meredith, Claire's granddaughter, alluded to mischief related to Claire's death. I would like to explore that subject and see what can be illuminated. I ask that no one take umbrage if the subject focuses on you, since my intent is to spread the exploration around..." she pauses and then adds, "perhaps to everyone in the apartment.

"I am certainly no detective; however, with the help of my brother and Meredith, and, of course, officer Hartunian, we have been trying to figure out what might have happened."

She pauses, turns to her right, and says, "This is Toni. She and her partner, the gentleman who left with Dr. Doolittle, are indeed officers of the law. They are collaborators in this...well, I guess we can call it...investigation.

"Some things simply do not add up. Claire was having headaches in the few weeks before her death, and we wanted to find out the triggers. Not sure if you all know this, but, when she passed, her body was found in the bathroom, on the floor, her death presumed to be, as it is so often with the elderly, a case of the body wearing out, natural, untainted by any treachery. As many of you do know, we consulted with you, at times asking rather obscure questions, gathering information from a myriad of sources, trying to piece together a pattern to give us direction.

"It has been frustrating, but, I hope, will turn out to be fruitful. Our thanks to all of you who responded so generously, for you certainly helped reveal much more than you realized."

She stops and moves about the room, as if permitting what she has said thus far to sink in. I am aware of Tommy Cox flexing his arms, not widely but within a small radius, in and out, in and out, a look of indifference on his face; in fact, his eyes are closed. Helen Cumberland is staring at the ceiling, lips scrunched together, either bored or affronted by the direction our gathering has taken.

Meredith taps me on the arm and tips her head toward the back row. Lenore Flores's face is like a death mask, pinched and bony; her dark brows are pulled down over her eyes, shimmering with tears.

Of all those present, Dr. Lyle Overstreet looks to be the most annoyed—at least as I read it. He is postured with crossed arms and a mouth turned downward, a scowl on his now clean-shaven face.

"A summary seems to be in order," Charlotte resumes, "and I

will start by going back in time, with Claire's California life. Some of what I say will be, perhaps, painfully blunt but truthful. This lovely, remarkable woman was a lesbian. She was also an atheist."

She stops to let her words be absorbed, aware that those in attendance are either knowledgeable about these facts, or learning of them for the first time.

"This information may have irritated some in this room. As a policewoman near Los Angeles, she was badly treated by some of the male officers. In fact, she was forced to file a lawsuit for harassment, which she ultimately won.

"Another woman, also on the police force, became Claire's life partner, and their relationship lasted for many years. Whether her blindness was the impetus for their romance to end is a moot question, though we do know that, after Claire's affliction had developed to the extreme, the partnership began to wither away, and thereafter came to an end.

"Through correspondence with her granddaughter, Claire negotiated the move to Bigelow Village and had lived here all these years until her recent death.

"Now, here is where the history gets murky, partly because Claire was so private, and partly because of attitudes she presumed existed among fellow residents and acquaintances.

"Claire was not a self-promoting person; she never tooted her own horn. What she believed, and how she lived and loved, were private matters. But there are those who cannot tolerate difference, no matter how discreet. It became clear to us, but not until after her death, that Claire and a person here in Pennsylvania were courting. In a moment, I shall give you evidence. For now, suffice it to say, she was involved in a romance.

"Any comments so far? We do welcome your reactions as a way to shine a brighter light on this whole, sad affair."

In a truculent voice, Helen Cumberland says, "I don't think I belong here. My connection was only to provide braille labels for Ms. Hazelton. I didn't know her in any other way."

"Ah, to be sure, Ms. Cumberland. However, if you don't mind, we would appreciate your presence, since the labels you provided are a key bit of evidence in what may have happened," Charlotte says, with an accommodating smile.

There is another quiet moment and Charlotte says, "Also, Double O, Oscar Ott, is in the same category—a supplier to residents here at Bigelow. In his case, prescription medicine and pills, which, unfortunately have turned out to be a corollary culprit in all this."

Elmore Hahn says rather loudly, "I like Trudy. She has a wooden cane."

Esther places her hand on her husband's arm and says, "Very nice, dear. Very nice."

"I'm kind of enjoying this," Tommy Cox says. "I read a murder-mystery book once, about a screwed-up family in the Middle East. Couldn't tell who done it until the last chapter."

Charlotte waits again, and, as she does, Augustus Hartunian strides into the crowded room. All heads turn, and he steps to the front.

"The old gal is dead all right. Doc Doolittle is going to schedule some tests with the forensic people to determine cause. The grandson was instructed to hold off on any burial plans." He realizes he may be butting in at some crucial point in the meeting, looks at Charlotte, and adds, "Sorry to interrupt."

This amuses me. The tough, professional officer deferring to the little-old-lady-amateur-sleuth.

"Thank you, Detective Hartunian," Charlotte says. "We are just about to canvass the room to try to explicate Claire's mysterious death."

She turns and begins. "Let us start with prescriptions. This concerns you, Dr. Overstreet. Much as you dismiss any intimation that your liberal dispensing of steroids for residents here is harmful, research we did proves otherwise. As probably most of us know, steroids are energizers and bulk builders, but, in excess and over time, they can cause hypoxia and restrict oxygen from reaching cell tissue. You know this and, I must say, persist in prescribing them. Partly because, alas, you have little respect for the elderly patients you serve."

Dr. Overstreet stands suddenly. "I don't have to take this crap. You certainly aren't a physician, and you don't know diddly about treating old folks with diminished energy."

"How about sitting down, Doc?" Hartunian says, an edge in his voice.

Charlotte cuts in, "I don't, Dr. Overstreet, but I have consulted with both a colleague of yours, Dr. Doolittle, and our pharmacist, Oscar Ott. My information comes from them."

His face pink and pulsing, Overstreet settles back in his chair, not a happy camper.

"Now, all that doesn't mean you are the culprit in this ugly scene," Charlotte says. "No one is presuming that you had any dire intent with your prescriptions, though, for someone who spends a good part of every week serving the elderly, you do have an intolerable attitude about them. I suggest you reexamine your values—either that, or reexamine your position here."

She stops, absorbs Overstreet's hostile glare, smiles at him, and resumes.

"We also learned that it is highly unlikely that the steroid build-up was the cause of Claire's death. Pharmacist Oscar Ott has assured us that she could have counteracted the poison intake with natural chelation elements that cleanse the blood. Chelates are compounds that whisk away accumulated plaque, largely in the form of metals such as calcium deposits. It was originally prescribed for children who suffered from lead poisoning as it clears the arteries.

"So, what could have been the cause?"

She looks over at Helen Cumberland. "You, Helen, as you revealed to us, suffer from fibromyalgia, a painful and chronic illness that can be treated with Zoloft, Prozac, or some other serotonin-releasing substance. You know, as do others in this room, that combining these powerful drugs with so-called natural remedies, such as St. John's wort, can be toxic. In fact, any excessive add-on can tip the scale and cause dizziness or even stroke.

"What we know—and listen carefully, all of you, to this— is that Claire had been taking a variety of meds and pills, including St. John's wort, and that she contacted Vision-Aide, Helen Cumberland's establishment, to obtain braille labels for her pill bottles. We also know that, on some of the pill containers, the labels had been tampered with, switched, if you will. You, Helen, came to her apartment about a week before her death, to deliver some labels."

"Oh, dear God, are you trying to imply that I did such a terrible thing? That I switched labels on the bottles?"

"Your fingerprints were not found on any of them, but then—as you and I know—you regularly wear rubber gloves, don't you?"

"Of course I do. I handle all kinds of harmful chemicals and the gloves are protection."

"What is suspicious is that, with your fibromyalgia, you are well aware of the danger of St. John's wort being added to a regimen of antidepressants. Besides that, you are a deeply religious person who believes that Claire's lack of religion was blasphemy. You even noted to us that she would be, in your frame of reference, punished after death, by…sorry to be so frank, going to hell."

"Exactly," Helen says, "and though we are not privileged to know the Lord's ways, I am convinced she will be, or has been, punished. But, surely you cannot believe that I would risk my own damnation by disobeying the commandment, 'Thou shalt not kill.' I would never think of living my life with such contradictions."

"Well, yes, I tend to agree with you. You are harsh and judgmental, and you have a narrow spectrum of tolerance for others who are different. However, as with Dr. Overstreet, I do not think you would deliberately set about to end another's life. But let us hold that possibility in abeyance for a few more minutes, even though it may be remote."

Ms. Cumberland looks disgruntled, her fingers busily playing with the large silver cross on her chest.

Okay, so far two attendees challenged and unhappy, but not positively accused. I anxiously wonder who Charlotte will address next.

She turns to her left. "Edith, you are another who has little tolerance for variant belief systems. Your orthodoxy is your own business, yet you disparage others who do not worship the way you do or, in Claire's case, do not worship at all.

"You are a doting wife, and Elmore is fortunate to have you ministering to his every need. Because of your vile language about disbelievers, others here at Bigelow latched on to you as the prime suspect in Claire's death, including Detective Hartunian here."

"Rubbish," Edith blurts out. "My life is guided by the commandments of Moses. My people only kill in self-defense."

"Good point—if true. However, I contend that one can debate when an act is in self-defense. In your case, the finger of suspicion was pointed at you, because, for a reason no one else seemed to know, you decided to steal a supply of St. John's wort from Freda."

Edith loses color in her face, and replies in a cracking voice, "She told me it helped with pain, and she left it sitting out when she walked away from her purse. I wanted to sample it. I planned to return the rest."

I pick up Edith's embarrassment. Her ethics are impugned, her pure-life motives challenged.

"Makes sense, but not to Freda. She assumed you were planting it in Claire's apartment—where the phony labels were already pasted on and where those pills would be erroneously consumed as something else."

"I didn't plant a thing. God knows I am not a bad person."

"Perhaps God does know that. As I see it, you are—the same as Helen here—a narrow person, unable to tolerate those who disagree with your life philosophy. It is a distressing thing, but, without a strong intervention of some kind, I doubt that you will change. I do agree, however, that you did not plant anything. I expect it will please you when I also say that I am convinced you are not the guilty party in Claire's homicide."

Another possible candidate dismissed. Charlotte is marvelously methodical in all this, and, one-by-one, the suspects are addressed—either chastised or cajoled—and labeled. So far, the labels have all been "innocent" of the crime. My head is spinning, since I have no idea where my sister will go next, and even less of an awareness of who the culprit truly is.

Others are equally uninformed, and, not surprisingly, the one who expresses it vocally is Freda.

"So, who is guilty? Do you know who is?" she shouts.

"Patience, Freda. All in good time."

Hartunian leans over and whispers to me, "I'm beginning to lose *my* patience."

"Oh, detective, I'm sure you are," I whisper back, "but you have to admit, this is fun."

29

DR. DOOLITTLE returns, and the interrogation process is held up for a few moments as he reports in.

"Trudy Langella passed away at 12:41 this afternoon. Dr. Segal notes that her heart could no longer accommodate the burden of blood distribution after the apparent stroke that felled her. Until we can run tests to determine what brought the episode on, it will be listed as a myocardial infarction, which is the death of a segment of heart muscle caused by a clot in the coronary artery."

Trying to be helpful, I'm sure, Dr. Overstreet speaks up. "A coronary blood clot will surely interrupt the blood supply."

"Yes," Doolittle agrees. "All that is pretty clear; what is not clear yet is what caused her to collapse."

"How's the grandson?" Charlotte asks.

"He seems rather calm about it. I believe he will be returning here shortly."

Doolittle settles back down as Charlotte turns to the group and says, "Since you asked, Freda, let's take a look at you for a minute."

Uh-oh, here comes another blast of hostility. I brace myself for what I expect will be Freda's raving retort.

"Sure, let's look at Freda, the perfect scapegoat. Point the finger at the one who speaks up, the one who rattles the cages. An easy target, aren't I?"

"I don't think so. You're proud of your iconoclasm, but that doesn't make you an evil person. I don't, for one minute, look at you that way."

Charlotte smiles sardonically and resumes. "A nuisance some-times, but not beyond redemption. In fact, I, for one, rather enjoy your cynical style. It is true that you also suffer from fibromyalgia, and are keenly aware of the toxic nature of mixing meds. But, with all that, I am also convinced that you are hardly one to sneak around altering labels on pill bottles."

Her whimsical mood seems to switch, suddenly, and she ad-dresses Freda with a grave tone, as if what is about to come is nothing to consider lightly.

"You do have your secrets, which, if we are to unravel this mys-tery, I'm afraid will have to be revealed. For example, there is the fact that you are originally from California, the same general area as was Claire. It is also a fact, known perhaps by a few people in this room, that there was a policeman, partnered with Claire, who, while sitting on a robbery stakeout, tried to sexually attack her. She managed to fight him off, and, in the ensuing exchange, the escaping perp was shot, but so was the cop–both killed. Claire came out okay, except for the disgusting betrayal by her own partner."

Freda's face is an ashen mask–stark as a wall, pale as egg white, lips pinched, brows creased like a lined sheet of paper.

"Nobody's business!" she shouts.

"True, but nevertheless it adds to our understanding of this ter-rible crime."

"I told you, Claire and I were friends. No secrets. We often talked about the asshole. Doesn't mean it matters now." Freda says this with a plea in her voice.

Detective Hartunian cannot restrain himself, and blurts out, "What asshole? Who you talking about?"

"In Claire's papers were some letters from years ago, exchanges with California folks who kept in touch with her." Charlotte stops, looks hard at Freda and says, "A couple were from Freda."

"So what?" Hartunian asks.

"Well, by now it might seem like an irony, but, after the at-tempted rapist was killed by the exchange of gunfire, his widow con-tacted Claire. They met, Claire disclosed what had happened, and the widow acknowledged that her husband had been a player and a cheat. She said she appreciated Claire sharing her story.

"That widow, ladies and gentlemen, is Freda Graham."

I, for one, am startled by this news. So, Freda joined Claire here at Bigelow, the two of them comrades with a common enemy, the dead husband-attacker. Neither had ever intimated that they knew each other from the past. What I wonder is, how much had Claire told Freda. Had she owned up to having shot the adulterating piece of crap? Was Freda in on Claire's secret, and was she, in a way, grateful for what Claire had done? I guess it makes no difference now that Claire is gone.

"Now," Charlotte says, "all of that is history, and it is prelude to another odd development—at least it may seem odd to some of us."

She turns her gaze over to the far corner of back-row seats.

"Not all of you know Lenore Flores." She gestures to a seated, startled, and frightened-looking Ms. Flores. "She has lived here at Bigelow for over two years and is a quiet person, pleasant as a spring shower, timid as an uncertain kitten.

"But, she is also a player in this complicated situation." She stops and directly addresses Lenore. "Aren't you?"

"I...I'm not sure. I didn't hurt Claire."

"That remains to be seen, but for now it would help to go over the background evidence. We know that Claire had a partner in California. That partner and she split up, presumably at the partner's behest after Claire's eyesight failed. It might have been equally sad for both of them, but, for Claire, the break-up ruptured a multi-year closeness, triggered her querying her granddaughter, and ultimately led to her relocating to Bigelow Village."

She reaches into her side pocket and pulls out a small blue paper, which I recall seeing her stash away without comment last time we searched for evidence in this very apartment.

"I would like to read from this note, written to Claire and dated a couple of years ago. 'Dear Claire: I still love you, you know. I am sorry that our separation was necessary. You had health problems and I became lonely and scared. If you are open to it, I would love to pick up with you again; I mean get back together. I know you have moved, but that is not an obstacle.' The note is signed—yes, it is signed with one word: 'Lenore.'"

I'm thinking, "Quoth the Raven, 'Nevermore,'" and the line, "Sorrow for the lost Lenore." So, Lenore is the long-time lover, and she followed Claire here—same as Freda.

Charlotte persists. "Someone had to read that to Claire—which we'll get to in a moment. Lenore, meanwhile, took the risky leap and moved to Bigelow, presumably to cancel out the estrangement and attempt to reconcile. But now I shall play Claire's response, recorded on a cassette tape. Obviously, she made a copy for herself, so, everybody, listen closely."

Charlotte reveals a small cassette player and pushes the 'play' button. Claire's voice, unmistakably firm, sounds clear and resonant. "Sorry, Lenore, but I have moved on. You're here now and I am certain it will be hard not to run into each other, but only as friends. You and I had lovely years. Everything changes."

"The questions that remain, folks, are these: Did Lenore take umbrage over the rejection? Was she perturbed enough to seek revenge? Or was she resigned to reside here, nearby Claire, and tolerate her former lover and partner taking up with someone else? And there is another question as well: Was it Freda who read Lenore's note for Claire? And a corollary—was and is Freda a closeted lesbian, fiercely jealous of Lenore?"

"Hell no!" Freda yells out. "And I wasn't her substitute lover, either."

I think, *thou dost protest too much*. Damn, what a cockamamie triangle!

"No, Freda. Nobody said you were," Charlotte replies. "But I'll lay you odds that, as Claire's friend, you dictated the note from Lenore."

"Reading for Claire wasn't a crime. She rarely needed help, but, when she asked for it, I was happy to do it."

"Okay, but you also resented Lenore, didn't you? As Claire's friend, you believed that Lenore had jilted her, walked away from the relationship, and no way did you want it to be resumed."

"Again, no crime in any of that. I told Claire that I thought she was correct in turning Lenore down."

"But you, Lenore," Charlotte says, "were not happy with Claire's reply. You hung around and watched, maybe even spied on her, trying to find out who her new lover might be."

"I…I didn't spy on her." Tears stream down Lenore's face and her shoulders shake with sobs.

"All right, you didn't spy. But it is clear you were desperate to know whom she chose in place of you. Were you pushed out of sorts enough to punish Claire? Maybe. You are a retiring sort of person, hardly assertive, and it would be out of character for you to become aggressive and openly punitive. Yet, you might have done the furtive thing, and methodically poisoned your former lover with the wrong combinations of pills."

"Oh, no," Lenore manages, between sobs, to blurt out. "I would never hurt her." She chokes for a moment, and says, "I still loved her."

"Disappointed in love," Charlotte says, "but carrying the torch."

"Yes, but there was nothing I could do. I had to accept her decision." Lenore's sobs increase and she places both hands over her face, head down toward her knees.

"Hmm, okay. I tend to agree with that. The spurned lover, hovering in the shadows, too distraught to do anything but watch…and suffer."

"But she brought it on herself," Jerry Romano says loudly. "She rejected Claire when her eyes went bad. She has no one but herself to blame for Claire turning her down."

Softly, Meredith says, almost in a whisper, "How come I didn't know any of this? Grandmother was certainly secretive about her relationships."

"My guess," I whisper back, "is that she didn't want to burden you with gory details. You knew most of her history, but her more current intrigues were better kept private."

Charlotte says, "We are beginning to unwind this whole, complex ball of string. A few more folks to query, and I think we may have ourselves a resolution."

"It's about time," Tommy Cox mutters.

I am aware that, in her clever way, and without concrete finger pointing, my sister has managed to chastise several folks about their attitudes. It doesn't mean any of them will change dramatically; change is slow and tedious, but, often in quiet moments, when seeds are planted, people begin to reflect on their styles. What remains, I am also aware, is to finally unmask the bad guy, man or woman, and let Detective Hartunian do his thing.

Charlotte resumes in a conversational tone, the passion with Lenore Flores set on a shelf for the moment.

"I want to mention our pharmacist, Oscar Ott, known to some of you as Double O. His insights have been invaluable in all of this. When we asked him about the effects of a build-up of steroids, he explained that it was unlikely that Dr. Overstreet's liberal prescriptions are what caused Claire's demise. He then introduced us to the relatively rare mineral called selenium, shown way back in 1996 to have, in small doses, a positive correlation with cancer prevention.

"We also learned, however, that an intake of excessive selenium, a dose as small as five milligrams per day, can lead to selenosis, which can be lethal for many humans.

"Selenium is a nonprescriptive trace element that can be bought over the counter in any drugstore or vitamin store. Dosage is presumed to be self-monitored—which, as we know, was more of a challenge for Claire because of her blindness. Oscar informed us that Claire periodically bought selenium as a health supplement. And, by the way, some studies in China have shown that selenium tends to be more abundant in rich shale soil, and foodstuffs grown in that soil have inadvertently been the prime source of accidental overdose.

"Now let us return to serotonin, a hormone produced naturally in the brain, which is a chemical messenger allowing different parts of one's brain to communicate with each other. In a practical sense, serotonin is responsible for helping the body regulate its mood, which is a good thing. However, too much serotonin in the bloodstream causes serotonin syndrome, which is on the increase in the United States. People who suffer from pain, depression, or fatigue often take drugs that release serotonin, but combining one such drug with another can cause this syndrome, which can trigger headaches and, as we mentioned earlier, strokes and even death.

"The autopsy shows that Claire's blood had an elevated amount of both St. John's wort, which, combined with another drug, could have brought on her stroke, and selenium, in high amounts deadly by itself."

Charlotte pauses only momentarily, as I see it, to underscore her next sentence.

"Either of those might have been what caused Claire to collapse and eventually...expire."

She stops to gauge the mood of those in the audience, her eyes panning the faces, her own face unfathomable. To me, Charlotte seems to be deliberately trying to look enigmatic, cagey, as if she has the ultimate secret. She seems to succeed in making most folks in the room feel uncomfortable.

At last she says bluntly, with finality, punctuating each word, "No doubt about it. Claire was deliberately poisoned by someone who switched the labels on her pill bottles."

30

DURING CHARLOTTE'S pause, Sam Capizi saunters back into Claire's apartment, seeming anything but sad, a jaunty look about him that I can't recall seeing in the past. If the information we have is correct, he stands to inherit a bundle from his grandmother's death. He sits quietly, as if trying to meld in with the crowd.

"Say, I'm a bit concerned about my merchandise out there," Delbert Kraus says. "The fellow monitoring my table is not a salesperson. How much longer do you figure this will take, Charlotte?"

"I am aware that we need to expedite the process. It shouldn't be much longer now, depending, of course, on how folks tend to answer the next several questions. Let me next mention our marvelous, healthy specimen: exercise coach Tommy Cox."

Tommy is on the alert, muscle-flexing on hold, eyes narrow and peering at Charlotte.

"Your leading of the folks in workouts is absolutely essential, and to be applauded. You didn't exactly appreciate Claire, who eschewed the exercise room's activities. I know, because you have had issues with me as well, since I keep fit in my own way and on my own time. None of that, however, could have aggravated you to the extent of being petty or vindictive. You would have no motive to want to hurt Claire, and, I apologize if this insults you, no sophistication in knowing how to mix or match meds."

"Hey, I'm no dummy. I can learn as fast as the next dude."

"Indeed," Charlotte says. "Suffice it to say, we know you are not the…uh…bad dude in all this. So, Tommy, you are off the hook."

He looks confused, yet shrugs noticeably, and settles back down, arms beginning again to flex and release, flex and release.

"Another wonderful helper in all this," Charlotte resumes, "is our friend, Wally Burt, whose café in New Hope is a gourmet's delight. On the counter, we have set out his marvelous baked goods, and his selection of wines as well. You are welcome to help yourselves again at any time.

"I have consulted with Wally at length, because I trust his affection for Claire and know that he has visited her here, in this apartment, several times in the past. He brought some of his pastries when he came—or at least that is what we thought, because we found a discarded pastry carton from his café in the trash basket. I also know that Wally assisted Claire with her meds, serving as the vision she was lacking, in an attempt to ensure the accuracy of her daily regimen. He had no way of knowing that the braille labels may have not reflected what was in the bottles.

"But he also used his eyes, or at least one good eye, eh, Wally, in an unplanned and most innocent way, to observe what was transpiring in the vicinity of his business establishment. In conversations with him, Wally revealed to me that, several times, he saw our dear Claire Hazelton chauffeured to and from his neighborhood by...no less than..." she stops, turns, and nods toward the Krauses, and finishes her sentence, "...Evangeline Kraus!"

"Oh," Evangeline manages, her head shaking from side to side.

Unfazed, Charlotte bores in. "There is, in Claire's closet, a chic stole, trimmed in faux fur. Sewn into its label in gold thread are the simple words, 'Enjoy—Eva.'

"Now, that tells us that Claire was better known to Evangeline, and likely to Delbert Kraus, than we have been led to believe." She looks piercingly at Evangeline's husband and asks, "Am I right, Del?"

"She came to our business off and on. Since she couldn't drive, Eva would volunteer to chauffeur her. I...don't see anything wrong in that."

"Of course not, a Good Samaritan activity. However, there was more to it than that, which I shall shortly explain.

"I said two things earlier which need to be reassessed. Let me hold off on one. As for the other, I said that the crumpled pastry box from Wally's café was confirmation that he had come to see Claire in this apartment. We already know that his fingerprints were on the pill bottles, since he had more than once helped Claire with her daily meds. Yes, Wally has been here, but, when I checked with him, he assured me that, despite several visits, he had never brought her pastries from his restaurant. So, my friends, someone else did."

Again, Charlotte pauses, this new information a surprise to Meredith and me, and a leap forward in the pursuit of another, different visitor. I think, *the noose is tightening.* More to the point, of all those in the room, who else might have visited Nutrition for The Heart-y, and purchased Wally's pastries to go? I recall Elmore, in all his innocence, stating that he liked Wally's place.

"Since," Charlotte continues, "we know that Evangeline Kraus had picked Claire up to bring her to and from her shop, it makes it rather likely that she was, at least on some occasions, a bearer of edible gifts. More specifically, the pastries from Wally's café.

"And yes, Wally has confirmed that the Krauses would periodically buy some of his goodies to take out. Note that I say the plural–*Krauses*–because both Delbert and Evangeline have done it. So perhaps, ladies and gentlemen, she was not the only one of this pair to visit Claire with goodies."

Suddenly Jerry Romano, the same Jerry Romano we saw observing us from an upstairs window, the same Jerry Romano who seems to keep a close tab on Charlotte, speaks out. "I can verify that. I often sit and read in the rattan lounges, both upstairs and down, just off the parking lot. Never thought much of it, but I saw each of them come here. Not together, mind you, but at different times. If I remember correctly, the woman made several visits, but the man only one."

"Imagine that–an eyewitness," Charlotte says. "Now I shall discuss the second item that needs to be reassessed.

"I said, several minutes ago, in no uncertain terms, 'Claire was deliberately poisoned by someone who switched the labels on her pill bottles.' It is true that some of the braille labels had been wrongly applied over the original prescription labels, and, if those mislabeled pills had indeed been dispensed in the wrong potencies, it could have caused Claire severe health issues. However, according to Dr. Doolittle, those increased dosages, when experienced, would have alerted Claire to some sort of error long before they would have caused her to lose consciousness and expire. We can only assume, then, that the faulty labeling was an error, either by Helen Cumberland, from Vision-Aid, or by someone trying to help Claire, but who couldn't read braille."

"I can assure you," Helen Cumberland speaks out, "that I made no such error. The vision patients from Bigelow Village do not always ask us to apply the labels. Yes, we print them up, but it would be a rare event for us to actually paste them onto the bottles."

"Yes," Charlotte replies at once, "understood. However, your last visit here was a bit over a week before Claire passed, and you admitted to having more than one patient to serve. Mistakes are made. But, hold on, before you pop a spring, let me add that we do not believe you did any deliberate mischief.

"The second item that I am correcting—and I wish to emphasize this—is that despite any pill bottle aberrations, Claire was *not poisoned* by any such error. I made my statement before, purposely to stir up feelings, which I think did happen. The pathetic fact is that Claire was indeed deliberately poisoned, however, in quite a different manner."

A palpable, collective shiver seems to pass through the assembly. I stare at Hartunian, whose face is furrowed and looks dour. I can only imagine that he must be bewildered by all these revelations and switchbacks. I also check out Evangeline Kraus, who, as Charlotte has shared with us, has chronically suffered from a mysterious depression.

Meredith touches my arm and whispers, "Evangeline Kraus looks miserable, and her husband not much better."

"The moving finger writes," I say, "and it seems about to settle on them."

"I wish to revisit one of the likely culprits in this poison scenario," Charlotte says. "Selenium. As mentioned earlier, it is a trace element known to be an effective antioxidant, but only in very tiny dosages. Excessive amounts are toxic and deadly. Claire's autopsy revealed a high level of selenium in her body.

"I skip now to what may seem an unrelated fact, but be patient and I will secure the connection. Commercially, the largest use of selenium worldwide is found in glass manufacturing, though it is also used in the drums of laser printers and copiers. Free selenium can be gleaned by processing the anode mud from copper refineries, or the mud from the lead chambers of sulfuric acid plants. Once processed, it can be sold to glass manufacturers, the industry with the most need.

"And I recently learned something interesting." She turns and faces Delbert Kraus. "Del, here, makes his own glass mannequins, which means he keeps on hand a supply of selenium. Am I right, Del?"

Delbert Kraus shrugs. "So? It's part of my business."

"Of course, and under normal circumstances, that is all you

would use it for. But, as you well know, in your life in the lovely tourist village of New Hope, circumstances have been anything but normal."

"Sorry to contradict," Delbert says, "but you know nothing about the circumstances in my private life."

"I know enough to raise some issues. For example, I know that Evangeline has been suffering from depression for many years. I also know a rather surprising piece of information: that her good friend, Claire Hazelton, a recipient of Medi-Care, would regularly procure antidepressants the likes of Prozac and Zoloft, and pass some on to Evangeline. Oscar Ott, good man that he is, questioned Claire as to why she needed those supplements. Honest Claire replied frankly that her good buddy needed them, but it would cost her so much more. Strictly speaking, that was not kosher, but Oscar never gave her an excess amount of anything. She may also, on occasion, have provided your wife with St. John's wort, though we have already established—and Claire knew—that one ought not to mix those meds.

"What was difficult to come up with was why you, Delbert, would have any reason to want to harm Claire. I struggled with that for quite a time, then, like an epiphany, it exploded in my thoughts when I was able to ruminate alone in the quiet woods."

"This is insanity!" Delbert says. "We have a small business and a modest life. My wife has not been at her best, but we have been working on that. Claire was one other person who tried to be helpful."

Charlotte walks over to Evangeline, stops in front of her, and says softly, "Your depression eased since you began to connect with Claire. She meant a lot to you, didn't she?"

Evangeline is sobbing, her head, as if palsied, continues to shake. At last she slowly lifts her sad eyes, looks up at Charlotte, and says, "She was a lovely person. We were close."

Charlotte waits, and, almost too softly for the rest of us to hear, answers, "Ah, but you were more than close. As Sinatra, sang, you had her under your skin."

"I suggest you leave my wife alone," Delbert says, rising from his chair. "This is harassment."

"Cool it, pal," Hartunian says. "Let the lady finish."

"We were both lonely," Evangeline whispers.

"Yes," Charlotte says, "no question that one can be lonely, whether alone, as was Claire, or paired with someone, as were you." She pauses only briefly, then adds, "You were...lonely in your marriage."

"She was not lonely. She was only depressed. She made mistakes!" Delbert shouts.

"Oh, Del, it wasn't a mistake."

Charlotte reaches into her pocket, pulls out a slip of paper, kneels down on one knee in front of Evangeline, and reads: "I am old, and young at heart; Second chances shine; I am woman with woman!"

A mournful animal cry escapes her as Evangeline leaps to her feet, turns, and begins to beat her head against the wall. Meredith rushes over and pulls her away, holding Evangeline firmly and tenderly.

I am painfully aware that these two very different women, for very different reasons, are big losers in Claire's death.

"Yes, yes," Evangeline cries out. "We were lovers! She was my soul mate."

She turns to her husband. "Del, I didn't want you to know. I didn't want to hurt you. When Claire died, it devastated me. She made my life so much richer."

"But, unfortunately," Charlotte says, "she didn't just die, and your husband *did* know."

Evangeline looks bewildered. Can it be, with all this, that she doesn't suspect something about her husband? This turn of events has me squirming in my pants. How do you clinch it, Charlotte?

31

THE SOLUTION to a crime is like the coda in a sym-
phony, everything building to a climactic moment, the denouement,
if you wish. For me, my sister had researched more than I could ever
have dreamed up. She methodically studied many possible suspects,
discarded what seemed to be obvious facts—such as the faulty labels
and the motives of people like Helen Cumberland and Esther Hahn—
and, along with the grateful wife of the dead cop, uncovered Claire's
secret lover from the past, both of whom are now residents at Bigelow.

I can't help but wonder how Detective Hartunian would have
done things differently. Here he is, present at this entire question-and-
answer event, and to his credit keeping relatively quiet, letting a rank
amateur sleuth do her thing. I make a mental note to ask him later
what he thinks.

As soon as Evangeline shouts out her confession, I scan the
room for reactions.

Freda, the uninhibited, in-your-face widow of the slain policeman, immediately stands and points at Evangeline. "Holy shit! So,
she's the new lover."

Timid and sadly frustrated, Lenore turns away from the group,
and, with her head down, facing the wall, she weeps.

I note that Jerry Romano has a satisfied look on his face and is
nodding either in acquiescence or outright approval.

Tommy Cox looks disgusted.

The two doctors appear to be avid spectators, showing neither surprise nor alarm.

Sam Capizi is mystified by the whole scene, and I wonder if, in the next week or so, his grandmother's autopsy will pin his young, conniving ass to the wall.

Oscar Ott, to his credit, goes to Lenore, placing his hand on her shoulder.

Wally, Charlotte's most helpful ally, looks stern, profoundly disappointed, I'm certain, in his New Hope neighbors.

And Helen Cumberland's mouth is pinched into a tight circle as she wiggles her head in disapproval, all the while fingering her silver cross.

I am bemused by Toni, who seems—except for a featureless look of satisfaction—unmoved by the entire affair. After all, the whole purpose behind police work is that crimes are to be solved.

Charlotte appears ready for the coup d'etat. Slowly, she walks about the room, turns, and faces Delbert Kraus from a distance.

"In many ways, Delbert, you are a good man. Your business is environmentally sensitive and your products are elegantly designed and turned out. You are both inventor and producer, skilled at the loom and sewing machine, and on the leading edge of fashion.

"Unfortunately, your wife of many years became distant, her chronic depression an increasing burden until, in desperation, she reached out for solace from another person. Though she may not have known that you knew about Claire, your injured spirit brought you to spy on her, follow her, and, in the end, use your plentiful skills and cleverness to rectify the situation."

"What are you saying?" Evangeline manages to ask. "What do you mean 'rectify the situation'?"

"With the help of the police lab, we were able to ascertain that several threatening notes, some sent to Claire and, later, to me as well, were comprised of printed letters cut out from the pages of the *New York Times*. Of course, the astute person who sent them off left no fingerprints.

"We know, Delbert, that you are a regular subscriber to the *Times*. In fact, while leaving Wally's restaurant one day, we greeted you from across the street and saw that you were reading just that newspaper."

"A million people read the *Times*." Delbert stops, and adds, "What is wrong with you people?"

"A lot is wrong with me, I admit," Charlotte says with a broad grin," but not when it comes to this information. Yes, the *New York Times* is widely read. However, fastidious as you are and were, the forensics people explained to Detective Hartunian that, apparently some shears used to cut the letters out of the *Times* were the same shears used to trim fabrics you utilize, containing faux fur, a few hairs of which were left lingering on the letters.

"Dear Detective Hartunian does not know you and so did not know what to make of this evidence. But, of course, when he shared it with me, it all fell into place.

"Here, in capsule form, is the entire sad story: You discovered that your wife was having an affair with Claire Hazelton, a woman, and followed her here for verification. A best guess is that you were humiliated by the situation and decided to eliminate the offending person."

"Eliminate...?" Evangeline sobs.

"Hold on one more minute, Evangeline. Your embittered husband, in sequential order, purchased a tray of pastries from Wally's café packed in a cardboard box; drove here to Claire's place by himself; told Claire he was delivering a gift from his wife, who was, he said, unable to deliver it herself; and drove off. In that gift, inserted into the pastries, was enough selenium to cause Claire's body to go into shock. She collapsed, and, after a time, expired from a severe stroke."

"My God! Del, is this true? You...you poisoned Claire?"

"Rubbish! Pure nonsense. She's making it all up."

Charlotte points a menacing finger at him. "As the youngsters say today, *you wish.*"

Evangeline, who has been standing against the wall, lunges at her husband, fingers made into claws. Toni is nearby and leaps in, grabbing Evangeline her around the chest and holding her firm.

Del Krause is weeping, fists clenched on his forehead, muttering what sounds to me like gibberish. The few words I can make out are "...can't be happening...bitch...ungrateful...." Hartunian strides toward Dell Krause, pulls the suspect's arms down and behind his back, and cuffs him. "You have the right..." he begins.

As Hartunian guides him out through the open apartment door, Krause turns his head and, over his shoulder, bellows back into the room, "That blind old witch was sabotaging my whole life!"

My sister stares after them, and says to an empty doorway, "You sabotaged your own life." She spins about and speaks to the assembly:

"It is tragic when any relationship falls apart; it means one wasn't paying attention."

Meredith says, "It only takes one."

To my surprise, Tommy Cox blurts out, "Let's hear it for the detective lady!" and starts a slow clap. Elmore Hahn, with a broad smile, picks up the cadence. The only other person to applaud openly is Jerry Romano, who says with gusto, "Bravo, Charlotte!"

In some ways, it is like a balloon that's suddenly had its air released. Our entire focus for the past several days has been on apprehending the evil person who ended Claire's life.

What we all now realize is that one need not be evil, nor, indeed, depraved, to be driven to do a reprehensible deed. Delbert Krause, as Charlotte said, was a good man as he lived through the variegated strands of his life—respected as a business entrepreneur, friendly in the community. He was driven to the brink by a perception of betrayal from his long-suffering wife and companion. Evangeline, as we have learned, had been miserable in the marriage, depressed to the point of self-pity. Claire gave her the one thing we all crave: hope.

—

The three of us are again in Charlotte's apartment. The merchant's fair is over—a smashing success for most vendors. Even Go Fur It, with its substitute monitor, came away with a profit. Wally's daughter, Jessica, reported a sell-out; all their pastries and wines purchased.

Some surprising developments have also come to our attention. Jerry "Romeo" Romano, some twenty-five years her senior, asked Antonia "Toni" Brown, Hartunian's assistant, on a date, and she agreed.

Lenore Flores, revving up her courage, asked Evangeline if she could drive her back to New Hope—both women, Claire's lovers. Both losers in her death.

Freda apparently apologized to Esther Hahn for suspecting her, though her nasty references to Jews can hardly be so easily discarded.

"What no one seemed to know," Charlotte says, philosophically, "was how abusive Delbert had been to Evangeline. Their marriage must have worked at one time, but, in the last few years, it was barely limping along. Wally told me that Eve would come to his café for coffee just about every day, and would mumble about her husband being unfeeling and distant. Her depression was a result of faded intimacy, a lack of physical contact, and a dreadful sense of being unloved."

"Yet," I say, "Delbert accused Claire of messing up his life. That implies he had to believe he was losing something valuable."

"Psychological abuse is everywhere," Meredith says. "It doesn't have to be physical. An abuser can be as charming as Prince Charming. But, when he perceives he no longer has the upper hand, his sense of privilege shaken and his *possession* slipping away, it can seem like his familiar life is being sabotaged."

"Good points, Meredith," Charlotte says. "In Delbert's case, there was a public face and a private face. To the world, he was the artistic, easy-going, pipe-smoking, successful entrepreneur, living in an enviable part of the world, partnered with a quiet but compatible wife, and fully enjoying his existence. But all that was built on keeping his partner compliant, and, in fact, docile. Eve became more like a humble servant than a wife."

"No wonder she looked elsewhere," I say.

"Well, in Eve's case, she turned to a woman," Meredith adds. "Homosexuality can be congenital, that is, built in at birth, but it can also be situational, such as in prisons."

"Nurturance doesn't balk at gender," I say. "I would guess that, in her unhappy state, Evangeline could have been tempted to connect with either a man or a woman."

"No way to be sure," Charlotte says. "Anyway, now that her conniving husband is out of the picture, she's the primary owner of a great little clothing store. It would behoove her to get her act together."

"What a weird twist," I let out. "Wouldn't it be a blast if our California transplant, Claire's former partner, shy little, shadowy, Lenore Flores decides to help her?"

"What about Sam Capizi?" Meredith asks.

"Hartunian cautioned him not to leave until the lab can determine if there was mischief in Trudy's death. The boy is kind of a backward character, and he may have lucked out financially in his grandmother's death. Or, he may be implicit in it. Time will tell."

"Hey, Sis," I say, "that may be your next caper."

"Bite your tongue!"

I look at Meredith and she looks at me. We have business to do. Charlotte looks at both of us and says, "Hey, this little escapade is over. Get the hell out of here."

"Nice way for an elderly lady-sleuth to talk," I say. After a pause, I smile at my own inner thoughts and add, "And one who doesn't pick her nose, either."

Charlotte and Meredith stare at me as if I were nuts.

32

IN MY RENTED apartment, Meredith and I sit on the edge of the queen-sized bed and laugh. It is late in the afternoon and shadows dance on the walls, a reflection of the few shuddering leaves from the Bigelow interior garden. Outside, the November chill persists, yet our inside nest is comfy and cozy–quite a contrast from Claire's unheated apartment.

I leave for LA late tomorrow afternoon, knowing our unfinished business is both delicious and burdensome. The unresolved question, prickly as a burr in a saddle, is how in hell are we ever going to resolve our persistent geographical dilemma?

Though we are laughing, it is not humor engendered. It is nervous laughter, spawned by the two elements of being alone together, with a glorious sense of freedom, and both of us being painfully aware of the transitory, therefore fragile, nature of our togetherness.

"What do you think, beautiful woman? How can we make a go of our relationship from three-thousand miles apart? I'm sort of stumped, and I would love it if you can help figure out what either of us can do about it."

Like a child staring at a parent for wisdom, I gaze at her, hoping she can devise a more astute solution than my meager resources are able to invoke. Meredith, as I see her, is more imaginative than I, her creative juices infinitely more elaborate.

"Hmm," she lets out, and adds, "I already have done something, but need to ask you a couple of questions first."

When she says this I think of Charlotte and her way of acting on a situation and keeping it private until the ripe moment. Seems that Meredith has learned a thing or two from my sister.

"Ask me anything," I say.

"What is your take on a person's career goals? I mean, in your estimation, does a man's profession have priority over a woman's? Are their work ambitions equally important? Or what?"

"I like to think I have no gender bias when it comes to work. In most cultures, women have been held down for too long. It's about time for them to have equal standing."

"Does that hold true in a partnership, a marriage, as well?"

I nod. "I'm so used to living alone that I have no expectations of a woman coming in and assuming the household duties. I've always taken care of my own cleaning, washing, cooking, and trash disposal. A life partner, which, with all my heart I hope you will be, would be a glorious addition, and I'd consider her work to be as vital as mine."

"I like your answers. I wanted to hear your perspective before I tell you what I've done."

"Hey, you're as mysterious as Charlotte."

"Not my intent, Greg. I only want to go into this whole thing with a clear view of the reasons why. You have to know in advance that I'm not willing to give up anything," she pauses for emphasis, then finishes her sentence a few decibels louder, "if the man thinks he's more entitled than the woman."

My hands are spread in supplication. No argument so far, with anything she's said, but her bottom line is yet to be laid down. Now I look at her imploringly, aware that I am desperate for this dilemma to be worked out.

We shift our positions on the queen-sized bed, and Meredith, almost as if this whole topic is easy as a walk in the park, lies back with her hands behind her head and gazes up at the ceiling.

"I'm still in the dark," I tell her.

"Last night, about seven o'clock our time, I went on the web and looked up the Los Angeles County Department of Social Services. Their agencies were all still open so I phoned the main office. I was informed that there are a few available social work positions. One, ironically, is located in Simi Valley, where my lovely grandmother was a cop for two dozen years. Now, Greg, I want you to hear what I am about to say with an open heart, because that's the spirit in which I am saying it. I am willing to consider giving up my position here, and relocating to the West Coast, but only if we are on equal footing and not because I believe your job is more important than mine."

"Meredith, I am…stunned, delighted, overwhelmed!"

"Don't get too excited. I haven't got the job yet. But wouldn't it be a kick, and certainly a tribute to my lovely grandmother, if I began helping oppressed families to recover in the same milieu where Claire served and protected the oppressed?"

"My home is only a twenty-five-minute drive from Simi Valley." I stop, and add, "That little city, which is actually across the line in Ventura County, has more cops living in it than any other in Southern California. Every year it appears in the top-twenty safest American cities list."

I stop again, annoyed at myself, and aware that I have been rattling off irrelevant information.

"Not sure if that cop statistic is a good or a bad thing," Meredith says, with a knowing smile.

"You wouldn't be living there, only doing your social work. My area is also considered safe, and I have all those wonderful orange trees. Besides, in my immediate area there are several quaint coffee houses, a mom-and-pop gift shop with the most unique kinds of merchandise, two Japanese restaurants with the greatest sashimi, a Chinese restaurant with to-die-for Won Ton soup, markets filled with fresh and even organic foods, and…"

Damn, there I go again, rattling off more trivia.

"Trying to sell me?" she interrupts.

"Yes. But I don't have to, truly. You'll love it."

She looks at me steadily, and says, "It would be nice to love it, but I'm beginning, more and more, to realize that…I love *you.*"

Words I haven't heard in years; words that drive me crazy.

"You do? So, what are you willing to do about it?"

"What do you have in mind?"

—

The next day, in the *Philadelphia Inquirer*, a small headline on the fourteenth page reads:

Elderly Amateur Sleuth Solves Murder

Local Detective, A. Hartunian, credits Bigelow Village resident, Charlotte Smart, with uncovering motive and method in poisoning death.

STAN CHARNOFSKY is a retired professor of psychology at California State University, Northridge (CSUN), where he taught for more than fifty years. But that's just the tip of the iceberg. In addition to his work at CSUN, Stan also writes books, and it could be said that his life reads like one.

Before teaching, in the 1950s Stan signed with the New York Yankees where he played in their farm system for six years. He later managed teams in Edmonton and St. Petersburg. Later still, Stan worked as the assistant coach at USC under the famous Rod Dedeaux, who was voted College Baseball Coach of the Century. Stan also served as head coach at CSUN from 1962-1966, with one championship team.

He was the founding director of the Educational Opportunities Program at CSUN (then known as Valley State College). Stan was inducted into the CSUN Athletic Hall of Fame in 2016. This was followed, in 2018, by his induction into the USC Baseball Alumni Hall of Fame. Stan is the former President (and a current board member) of the National Association for Humanistic Psychology. In 2016, Stan received the Distinguished Teaching Award at CSUN.

And of course Stan writes books. His numerous publications include *When Women Leave Men: How Men Feel, How Men Heal* (New World Library) and *The Deceived Society* (Trafford). Stan resides in Northridge, California.